Three French Hens and a Murder

A Charlie Kingsley Novella

Books and series by Michele Pariza Wacek

Charlie Kingsley Mysteries
(Cozy Mysteries)
See all of Charlie's adventures here.
https://MPWNovels.com/r/ck_3fh

Redemption Detective Agency
(Cozy Mysteries)
A spin-off from the Charlie Kingsley series.
https://MPWNovels.com/r/da_3fh

Secrets of Redemption series
(Pychological Thrillers)
The flagship series that started it all.
https://MPWnovels.com/r/rd_3fh

Mysteries of Redemption
(Psychological Thrillers)
A spin-off from the Secrets of Redemption series.
https://MPWnovels.com/r/mr_3fh

Riverview Mysteries
(standalone Pychological Thrillers)
These stories take place in Riverview, which is near Redemption.
https://MPWnovels.com/r/rm_3fh

Three French Hens and a Murder

A Charley Kingsley Novella

by Michele Pariza Wacek

ISBN 979-8-89351-000-3

For my family, for always believing in me.

Chapter 1

"Watch out!" Pat yelled as I swerved to miss the oncoming car that had drifted across the center line. Although to be fair, with all the snow, it was difficult to see the center line. The car skidded, and for a heart-dropping moment, I was sure I was about to lose control and go careening off into a snowbank on the side of the road. But then I felt the tires regain their grip and the car was under my control again.

"Stay in your lane," Pat yelled as we passed that other car, although it was doubtful the driver heard her with our windows up. Tiki, Pat's miniature poodle, yelped as well. She was dressed in a festive green sweater with a sparkling Christmas tree on the front and matching green ribbons. She looked up at me with her black eyes and gave me a quick tail wag. Unlike Pat, who was bracing herself against the dashboard, Tiki appeared to be enjoying the excitement.

"You think if you lived in Wisconsin, you would know how to drive in the snow," Pat said.

"Well, it is the first real snow of the season," I said.

"That's no excuse," Pat said. "It's like riding a bike. You don't forget." She glared as another car fishtailed as it turned onto a side street. "Maybe this wasn't such a good idea after all."

I refrained from pointing out it was her idea, and if it had been up to me, we would still be in my nice warm kitchen, eating cookies and drinking tea.

We had spent the morning at Redemption's senior center, helping put up Christmas decorations. The original plan, which Pat was also using as a bribe to get me to come with her, was after we finished decorating, we would treat ourselves to lunch at Aunt May's, and then I would finish dropping off my tea deliveries while Pat and Tiki kept me company. I had a small custom tea business I ran out of my house, growing herbs and flowers in my backyard for my teas, and a couple of times a week I would run around Redemption making deliveries. Just as long as the weather cooperated, that is.

Which it absolutely wasn't today. The snow had started innocently enough as we hung tinsel and garland in the main activity hall, just a few flakes floating down from the sky. I hadn't thought it would be that big of a deal, but then, the next time I glanced out the window, it was looking more serious. The snow was falling in thick sheets and had begun to accumulate. By the time Pat and I hiked our way out to the car, it was starting to resemble a blizzard.

"At least we finished up the senior center," I said, peering out the windshield as the wipers furiously pushed the snow out of the way. "That's one less thing to worry about."

"I suppose that's true," Pat said, frowning at the snow. Pat was one of my first tea customers and had also become one of my best friends. She was a good decade or so older than me, and the best way to describe her was round. She was plump with a round face, round black-rimmed glasses and short, no-nonsense brown hair that was turning gray. "And it's not like we would have known sooner. The weather forecast was supposed to be sunny and clear, maybe a few snow showers late this afternoon. Absolutely nothing like this."

As if to emphasize that the weatherman was a liar, the snow seemed to fall even harder. I gently tapped the brake, even though I was already driving so slow I was practically crawling. "It is weird. But it is Redemption."

"Redemption has plenty of strange things, but the weather tends to not be one of them," Pat said.

Redemption, Wisconsin, had a long reputation of peculiar and unexplained events that had happened over the years, starting in 1888 when all the adults disappeared one day, leaving only the children. No one knew what happened to the adults. The children all claimed when they went to bed, the adults were there, and when they woke up in the morning, they were gone.

The adults may have been the first to have gone missing, but they weren't the last. Over the years, Redemption had far more disappearances than what would be considered normal for a town its size, along with plenty of other odd occurrences such as ghosts, hauntings, and murder.

Suddenly, Pat sat up and pointed "Hey, is that ... *Santa* over there?"

I glanced toward the side of the road. There was a man there, dressed in what looked like a red Santa outfit complete with a hat, although it was hard to tell with all the snowflakes whipping around him.

"It sure looks like it," I said. "Although I wonder what he's doing on the side of the road. He's not anywhere near the mall."

"He also doesn't look very good," Pat said.

Pat was right. Santa seemed to be tottering confusedly in a circle, like he wasn't sure which way he was supposed to go.

"Do you think he's lost?" I asked.

Pat snorted "Who wouldn't be lost in this snowstorm?"

"He's not wearing a coat," I said. "Maybe we should see if he needs a ride."

As soon as the words left my mouth, Santa paused in midstep and then collapsed, falling backward into a snowdrift, his legs and arms stretched out like a starfish.

"Ack!" Pat said. "Maybe he really IS hurt."

"Or he's having a heart attack or a stroke," I said, turning on my signal and easing over to the side of the road, practically driving into a snowdrift myself in order to get over far enough. The car behind me let out a loud beep.

"Are you kidding me?" Pat fumed, glaring at the driver behind us. "It's Santa! Where is their Christmas spirit?"

"They're definitely going to be on the naughty list," I said, carefully getting out of the car and praying neither I, my car, nor Pat got hit.

The wind had picked up, swirling around us and nearly tearing the car door out of my hands before I could close it. My skin prickled as the tiny ice crystals pelted it. I bent over, shielding my face against the worst of the wind, and slipped and slid over to the man.

"Are you okay?" I asked. He had managed to sit up and was leaning on the snowdrift behind him, a befuddled expression on his face. Now that I was closer, I could see he took being a Santa very seriously. His long white beard and bushy white eyebrows looked natural. I wondered if he dyed them white. His red hat had fallen askew across his forehead, almost covering one of his eyes. His glasses were perched crookedly on his nose, which was unusually red and puffy.

He blinked confusedly at me. "What happened?"

"You fell in a snowbank," I said, bending down to try and examine him, although it was difficult to do with the snow coming down so hard. "Do you think you can stand up?"

He looked around, as if just realizing where he was. "I'm not sure. Have you seen my French hens?"

"French hens?" I asked, wondering if I heard him right. The wind was whistling loudly by my ears, not to mention Pat was muttering curses under her breath as she shuffled her way toward us.

He squinted as he looked around. "They were just here."

I looked around as well but didn't see anything but snow and more snow. "Pat, did you see any French hens?"

Pat looked at me like I had lost my mind. "Did you say French *hens*? Like birds?" She flapped her arms as if they were wings.

"They're always wandering away," Santa sighed.

I shot Pat a concerned look. Either we were going to have to start searching for a couple of frozen birds, or Santa had a head injury. Taking a closer look at him, I did see what looked like dried blood on the white fur trim on both his hat and his coat, but no obvious cuts.

"We better get him to a hospital," I said to Pat. "Think you can lift him?"

She shot me a look, at least I think she did, the snow made it difficult to see, as she skidded over to Santa's other side. "I can try."

"Oh, you two girls shouldn't be doing this," he protested as we each took an arm. "That's a job for my elves."

Elves? He must be joking. Or he hit his head so hard he really thought he was Santa Claus. "We've got this," I said as we started hauling him to his feet. "We're stronger than we look."

"Speak for yourself," Pat huffed.

After a lot of pulling and pushing, and almost falling not once, but twice, we finally got Santa up. "Can you walk?" I asked him.

He blinked again and adjusted his glasses. "Walk? Where do I need to walk to?"

"My car," I pointed toward it, wincing as I noticed the amount of snow and slush around it. I hoped I wasn't stuck.

He stared bewilderedly at my car. "Your car? Why are we doing that? Where's my sleigh?"

"Your sleigh?" This had to be a joke. "What kind of sleigh?"

He waved his hands. "You know. The kind you ride in. Oh drat, where did those elves go? They would know where the sleigh is."

"Maybe they're with the French hens," Pat said drily.

He swiveled his head around to face her. "Oh, you're right. That's probably exactly where they are." He shook his head. "I'm going to have to have a conversation with them. They shouldn't be taking the sleigh out without me."

"Good idea," I said, as we half led, half dragged him toward the car. "But for now, let's get you in the car."

"I don't think you're going to be able to find my sleigh in a car," he said doubtfully, although he appeared to be coming along mostly willingly. "My sleigh is … special. It can go places a car can't."

"Well, as I don't have a sleigh, we'll have to make do with my car," I said, as I fumbled for my keys. Tiki was standing up in the front seat, excitedly pawing at the side window. Santa paused when he saw her.

"Oh, look at the little sweetheart," he said, bending closer to the window and wiggling his fingers. "Hello there. Have you been a good little girl?"

Tiki's tail was waving furiously.

He chuckled, a deep, low noise that sounded suspiciously like he was saying ho, ho, ho. "I think that's a yes."

"Here we go," I said, getting the back door open finally and practically pushing Santa into the back seat. Once he was safely tucked inside, Pat got into the front, and I went around to the driver's seat. Tiki stood on her hind legs, trying to greet Santa, who chuckled again as he leaned forward to rub under her chin.

"By the way, I'm Charlie," I said, putting the key in the ignition. "And this is Pat."

"Yes, I know," Santa said.

I eyed Pat who rolled her eyes. "And you are…"

"You know who I am," Santa said. "We met once before, remember?"

"You mean at the shopping mall?" Pat asked.

"I don't do shopping malls," Santa said. "Do you think I have time for that? Other men, very fine men I might add, take care of that."

"Then how did we meet if you're not sitting in shopping malls?" Pat asked, before snapping her fingers. "Oh wait. I know. You played Santa a few years ago in that Christmas play, didn't you?"

"That was yet another fine man, who is also quite a talented actor, but also not me," Santa said.

"Then how did we meet?" Pat asked.

"I wasn't talking about you, I was talking about Charlie," Santa said.

"Me?" I whirled around in my seat to face him. "When did we meet? Was it back in New York?" I was mentally flipping through my memories trying to remember meeting a man who looked like Santa Claus. Was it at one of my parents' parties?

Santa smiled kindly at me. "Oh no. Don't you remember? You were very helpful."

Helpful. That word triggered something, an almost memory, a

tiny, fragile image that floated teasingly just out of reach.

I opened my mouth to ask another question, but then Pat shivered. "Can we at least turn the heater on? It's freezing in here."

"It's not freezing in here at all," Santa said, although I noticed his teeth were chattering, and his lips were turning a light shade of blue. "If you want to talk about freezing, let's talk about the temperatures at the North Pole. Or traveling in a flying sleigh in winter in the middle of the night."

"That would be cold," I said as I turned the key to start the car. As much as I wanted to ask Santa more questions about exactly what he meant about meeting me, I knew it would need to wait. His eyes had started to glaze over again, and his skin was turning an unhealthy color. He didn't need questions, he needed a hospital. I twisted the heat to full blast, even though the engine hadn't quite warmed up enough.

"I agree, but that doesn't mean we have to suffer in a cold car," Pat said, rubbing her mittened hands together.

"I suppose that's true," Santa said, leaning over to peer out of the window as I began to pull into traffic, praying I wouldn't slide into anything. "And who knows how long it will take to find my sleigh, so we might as well be comfortable." He frowned, like he disapproved at the sight before him. "I'm sure the elves were just trying to help, but it's vexing that my sleigh is nowhere to be found. I'm not even sure where to tell you to start looking."

"That's okay," I said as I carefully pressed down the gas pedal and tried to calculate the fastest route. "We should first take you to the hospital and get you checked out."

"The hospital?" His voice was puzzled. "Whatever for?"

"We need to make sure you're not seriously hurt," I said.

"That's ridiculous." He let out that chuckle again. "You can't hurt Santa!"

"Well, we did find you in a snowbank in the middle of a snowstorm," Pat said. "That's not exactly normal behavior."

"And you have blood on your clothes," I added.

"Blood?" He peered at his outfit, adjusting his glasses. "Oh, look at that. I wonder where that came from?"

"That's why we should get you checked out," I said.

"I hope it's not from the French hens," he fretted. "I really wish I knew where they were."

I flipped on my signal light and eased my way into a turn. "Do you remember what happened?"

He rubbed his head. "The last thing I remember was Dremel yelling to watch out."

"Dremel?"

"One of the elves," he explained. "He was the one driving. I think." He rubbed his head, his eyes getting that glassy look again. "It's all very fuzzy."

Pat and I exchanged another worried look. "I didn't see another car accident anywhere," Pat said in a low voice. "Do you think he walked here from somewhere?"

"He couldn't have walked that far," I said, thinking about the heavy snowdrifts and how badly he had been stumbling.

"I'm fine," Santa said again. "I told you; you can't hurt Santa."

I thought about asking how he explained the blood on his clothes but decided not to bother.

"So Dremel," Pat said. "He's one of your elves?"

"One of my best," Santa said proudly. "He's so dependable and trustworthy. I never worry if he's involved. That's why I'm hoping he's the one taking care of the French hens. Otherwise, who knows what's going to happen to them."

"Is there also a partridge in a pear tree somewhere?" Pat asked.

"Of course not," Santa said. "Do you have any idea how heavy a full-grown pear tree is?"

"I would suspect pretty heavy," I said, as I turned into the parking lot of the hospital.

"Exactly," Santa said.

The parking lot was packed, but we lucked out as someone pulled out near the entrance right as we drove up. As soon as I parked, I hurried out of the car to help Santa out.

"I still think this is silly," he grumbled as I half pulled, half pushed him out of the back seat. "We have so many other things to do, we don't need to be wasting time here."

"Humor me," I said, trying not to grunt from the effort.

Tiki was still jumping up and down on the front seat, trying to give Santa a kiss. He laughed and reached over to rub her chin. "You be good, Tiki. I'll see you soon."

Tiki danced around as Pat and I looked at each other in confusion. "Did we tell you her name was Tiki?" Pat asked.

Santa straightened up and winked at us. "You must have. How else would I have known it?"

Chapter 2

I wasn't sure how the hospital staff would react to us bringing in a man in a Santa suit who told everyone to either call him Santa or Kris (whichever would make them more comfortable, he would even answer to Nick if that was preferable) but to everyone's credit, they didn't miss a beat. "I don't suppose you have any identification on you," the woman checking us in asked. Her hair was dyed black, and she had a pair of tortoise-shell glasses perched on her nose.

"Why would I carry identification? Everyone knows who I am," Santa said.

Her eyes cut over to me.

"We found him on the side of the road like this," I said. "I didn't see a wallet anywhere."

"That's because I don't carry a wallet," Santa said.

"Okay, then," the woman said, making a note on the form. "Take a seat in the waiting room, and a nurse will be out to see you shortly."

"Thank you, Jeannie. You've been very helpful. And very good as well, haven't you?" Santa said heaving himself out of his chair as Jeannie looked a little nonplussed.

"How did you know her name?" I asked Santa.

He grinned and gestured at her chest. "Why she's wearing a name tag. Don't you see it?"

I glanced at Jeannie, and sure enough, she was wearing a name tag. A very small and subtle one, made of silver with black writing. I could barely make out the letters, even if I squinted, and I had twenty-twenty eyesight and was a good fifty years younger than Santa was. I looked back at him, and he smiled one of his beatific smiles at me before wandering toward the waiting room.

"Maybe it's his glasses," Pat said doubtfully, also staring at the name tag.

"Maybe," I said.

"I wonder if he would give me the name of his eye doctor," Jeannie mused, adjusting her own glasses.

"I was wondering the same," Pat said. Jeannie flashed her a quick smile before calling up the next person waiting.

"How long do you think we should stay?" Pat asked as we watched Santa meander through the waiting room.

"Um … I'm not sure," I said. Santa had paused to chat with a small girl holding her arm awkwardly across her chest. Her face was streaked with tears, but she was smiling at whatever Santa was saying to her. "I guess I was thinking we'd wait until after he was seen by a doctor."

"Yeah, but it's kind of weird, isn't it?" Pat said as Santa bent over and pretended to pull a coin out of the little girl's ear. "Us hanging around? It's not like we actually know who he is. Although…" she gave me a sideways glance. "He sure seems convinced you two met before."

"Well, he also seems convinced there are French hens and elves wandering around Redemption," I said, trying to sound less concerned than I felt. That almost memory continued to tantalize me, but every time I reached for it to drag it into the light, it melted into the darkness of my subconscious.

"Not to mention a sleigh," Pat said, then wrinkled her forehead. "What do you think the difference is between a French hen and a regular hen?"

"Maybe the French hens wear berets and cluck in French," I

said.

"Oui, oui," Pat said with a quick grin. "But seriously, what are we doing here? He's a stranger. The doctors should be able to take care of him now, right? Plus, I don't want to leave Tiki too long out in the car. I know you left the car running for her, but still."

"Tiki will be fine," I said. Not only had I left the car running and the window cracked for fresh air, but Tiki also had several blankets she could burrow in if she got cold. "Maybe we just stay long enough to hear what the doctor says. I agree, he should be in good hands now, but I don't know. He's all alone. Should we really just leave him?"

"He's not alone. Dremel is out there somewhere," Pat said. "Along with his sleigh and his French hens."

"I doubt the French hens would be much help in this situation," I said.

"Or the sleigh," Pat said, as Santa threw his head back and let out a loud ho, ho, ho. "But, yeah, it does feel like we'd be abandoning a child on some level, doesn't it?"

"Santa?" A nurse called out. "We're ready for you."

Santa stood up. "Oh. That's me!"

"Of course it is," the nurse sighed as Pat and I walked toward Santa. She looked us up and down. "Are you family?"

"They might as well be family," Santa said. "They've been taking excellent care of me." He winked at both of us.

"We'll stay out here and wait for you," I said.

"Nonsense," Santa said, while at the same time the nurse said "You don't have to. If he doesn't mind, we don't."

I glanced at Pat, who arched her eyebrows at me.

"Come along," Santa said as he headed toward the door that

led to the examining rooms. "We don't want to keep the doctor waiting."

"No, I guess we don't," I said, as Pat and I hurried to catch up.

* * *

"So, does he normally think he's Santa?" Dr. Emil asked. He was short and portly, with a shiny balding head and kind eyes. We were standing in the hallway outside of the examining room. Nurses and orderlies walked by us as we huddled by the door, the soles of their shoes squeaking on the linoleum. It smelled like bleach and other harsh chemicals.

Santa was still in the room with the door closed, presumably to keep him from hearing us. Or maybe to keep him from wandering away.

"I haven't a clue," I said. "We found him on the side of the road."

Dr. Emil peered at us over his glasses. "You found him like this?"

"Yes, he didn't look right, so we stopped," Pat said.

"He wasn't walking right, and then he just fell into the snow," I said.

Dr. Emil frowned and made a note in his chart. "Did he lose consciousness?"

"No. He was just … confused." I flapped my hands. "Talking about missing French hens and sleighs. We assumed he was in a car wreck."

"Did you see the car wreck?"

"No, but that seems to be the most likely explanation, as the last thing he remembers is the elf yelling 'watch out,'" Pat said.

Dr. Emil raised an eyebrow. "Elf?"

"Dremel," I said. "One of his top elves."

"I thought he said one of his best," Pat said.

"Oh, maybe you're right," I said.

Dr. Emil's eyes darted between us. "So, the elf was driving and got into an accident?"

"That's how it sounded," I said.

"And there was no one else with him? Elves or otherwise?"

"He was alone," I said. "Not an elf or a French hen in sight."

Dr. Emil tapped his pen against the file. "Hmm."

I glanced at Pat. "What's hmm? Is there something seriously wrong with him?"

Dr. Emil shook his head. "As far as I can tell, no. He has a rather nasty looking bump on his forehead and a mild concussion, which appears to be the worst of his symptoms."

"What about the blood?" Pat asked.

"He had a nosebleed as well, although it's odd there wasn't more blood on his face. The snow must have washed it off."

"I guess that makes sense," I said. "Noses can bleed a lot. Although it's weird that some of the stains were pretty far down his outfit."

"It's also possible that some of the blood wasn't his as well," Dr. Emil said.

Pat's eyes went wide. "Oh no! The French hens! Can you tell if the blood was from a bird or not?"

"Or an elf?" I asked.

"Not without sending it in for tests," Dr. Emil said. "It would probably be easier and quicker to find the source of the accident."

"Oh, I hope those French hens are okay," Pat said, shaking her head.

"Do you know if there have been any accidents reported?" I asked. "The snow is still coming down hard out there, so I don't want to be driving any more than I have to."

Dr. Emil straightened his glasses. "I'm sure there have been lots of accidents reported. When the weather is this bad, there's going to be a lot of fender benders and cars in ditches. It's going to take some time to sort out the serious accidents from the minor ones. Which leads me to my next point." He hesitated, glancing toward the closed door.

I started to get a bad feeling. "What point?"

Dr. Emil turned to us, shifting from one foot to another, an almost embarrassed expression on his face. "Well, there's no medical reason to admit Santa in the hospital. He'll have a bad headache for the next couple of days and he ought to have someone keep an eye on him with the concussion, but otherwise, he's fine."

"He thinks he's Santa," Pat said.

"A temporary problem," Dr. Emil said. "My guess is in a day or two, his memory will return."

"But, it doesn't sound like a memory issue," I said. "It sounds like he thinks he's Santa, not that he doesn't remember who he is."

Dr. Emil waved his hands. "Minor detail. My guess is he has temporary amnesia, caused by the head injury. And as he saw he was wearing a Santa suit, he decided he must be Santa."

Pat and I eyed each other. "But … he would know Santa doesn't exist, right?" I asked. "Even if he doesn't know who he is, he wouldn't assume he's a fictional character. Right?"

"Head injuries can be unpredictable," Dr. Emil said, which

didn't exactly answer the question. "But, the fact he does seem a little more confused than we typically see with head injuries, I think it would be wise if he wasn't simply discharged, especially in this weather, with nowhere to go and no one to look after him. The cops have their hands full right now with the weather, so our hands are tied."

Dr. Emil gave us both a meaningful look. Pat and I looked at each other again.

"Are you saying you want one of us to take him in?" I asked cautiously.

Dr. Emil looked relieved. "Could you? That would be a huge help. And it should only be for a day or two. Once he regains his memory, he should be fine."

"But, what if it takes longer than a day or two?" I asked. "As you said, head injuries are unpredictable."

"That's true, but it's highly uncommon for temporary amnesia to last more than a few days," Dr. Emil said. "But, in the rare case it does, the cops should have gotten through their backlog of cases and would have time to investigate who he is and where he came from. With any luck, they also would have found the accident site."

"I don't know…" Pat said, staring at me. I could almost feel her eyes burning into my head, trying to convince me to say no. She knew I was a sucker for stories like these. "He IS a stranger. We don't know anything about him."

Dr. Emil adjusted his glasses. "While I would agree with you under normal circumstances, these aren't normal circumstances. You wouldn't want him wandering around in the middle of a snowstorm, would you?"

"I suppose not," I said with a sigh.

Pat shook her head. "I can just hear Wyle now."

I winced as Dr. Emil gave us a curious look. "Wyle?"

"Just a friend," I said, glaring at Pat, who gave me an innocent smile in return.

Officer Brandon Wyle *was* just a friend, despite what Pat and everyone else seemed to think. Sure there might be a little flirting between us, but it didn't mean anything. Friends could flirt. Besides, even if there was something between us, I wasn't interested in a relationship.

But Pat *was* right that Wyle wouldn't be at all pleased with me bringing Santa home. He wasn't a huge fan when I got involved in criminal investigations, as he was a strong believer that the professionals should be the ones investigating, not tea makers. While I agreed with him in theory, it wasn't practical in practice, as I had not only discovered I had a knack for sleuthing, but my tea clients also had a knack for getting into trouble and needing my sleuthing skills.

Because Wyle was more interested in solving cases than ego trips, he begrudgingly accepted my help. However, I had a feeling he wouldn't have the same reaction to me bringing home a complete stranger, even a stranger who may also need my sleuthing skills in the future.

"Oh, well, I'm sure once your friend hears all the details, he'll understand," Dr. Emil said.

"I wouldn't be so sure of that," Pat said, but Dr. Emil kept going like he hadn't heard her.

"Since that's settled," he said, closing the file firmly and tucking it under his arm. "I'll pull together his paperwork, so he can be discharged."

The door to the waiting room opened, and Santa poked his head out, his red hat drooping over one of his eyes. "Are we ready to go to Charlie's house yet?"

Chapter 3

I slid a sheet tray of rolled out sugar cookies shaped like snow-men and Santas (in honor of my unexpected guest) into the oven and closed the door. The coffee cake I had made earlier was cooling on the counter, and once I finished cutting out the rest of the cookies, I would start the bacon and egg casserole I had planned for breakfast.

But before I did any of that, I was taking a break and having a cup of tea.

The morning sun was peeking over the horizon, revealing a winter wonderland. The pristine white snow sparkled in the sun, like glittering little diamonds. Midnight, my black cat, was curled up on his favorite chair, and the kitchen smelled like cinnamon, sugar, and coffee. It would have been a lovely, relaxing morning, if I wasn't consumed by thoughts about my aforementioned guest.

Although, so far, it had been remarkably uneventful. Yester-day, Pat had insisted on staying with me for much of the after-noon and evening, even though Santa had been so exhausted he could barely keep his eyes open. Once he had greeted Midnight, my black cat, by name (even though I was positive I hadn't said anything about owning a cat, much less what the cat's name was) I got him settled into his bedroom with a cup of tea and some cookies. By the time I brought him a tray for dinner, he was sound asleep. I still left him the meal, in case he woke up in the middle of the night and was hungry.

Pat not only stayed for dinner but had called her husband Richard to come over and eat with us. While I appreciated the company, it ended up being a less than pleasant experience. Richard spent most of the meal grilling us on the dangers of stopping for strangers, especially strangers who appear to be hurt. "It could have been an act," he kept saying.

"It wasn't an act," Pat said. "The doctor said he had a concussion."

"A mild concussion," Richard said. "And you're letting him sleep."

"The doctor said it was okay just as long as I keep an eye on him," I said. "He's an old man, he needs his sleep."

Richard grunted. "That old man could rob you blind in the middle of the night, and then what are you going to do?"

"Santa wouldn't do that," Pat said. "Santa leaves presents, he doesn't take them."

Richard did not look amused.

Even though Pat defended me to Richard, I could tell she was worried about me when she made me promise to call the moment anything changed with Santa. I suspected it was less about concern for Santa and more about making sure I was okay.

And despite me assuring both of them I would be fine, I ended up not sleeping all that well myself. Between checking on him every few hours—as all I could think about was how dreadful it would be if something happened to Santa on my watch—and trying to capture that elusive memory of where we met, I barely got any rest. Finally, I decided I had done enough tossing and turning and figured I might as well get an early start on my baking.

With Santa around, I was probably going to need a lot more cookies than normal.

I had just finished my tea and was considering pouring myself a cup of coffee—I only drank coffee on days where I didn't get much sleep the night before, and today definitely qualified—

when there was a loud knock on the door.

It must be Pat checking on me, although it was a little early for her. And usually, she would call before coming over. But maybe she was sufficiently concerned about the situation she decided to just pop on by.

But it wasn't Pat. It was Wyle. And he didn't look happy.

I stared at him through the peephole, as I raked a hand through my wild, brownish, blondish hair. I wondered if I had enough time to run upstairs and change into something a little more becoming than my gray sweatpants, fluffy pink slippers, and a matching pink sweatshirt that really needed to be thrown away as it had a big stain across the front. Maybe I could even take a moment to add some mascara and eye liner around my hazel eyes as well … but then Wyle started pounding on the door, and I figured I better open it, stained sweatshirt and all.

"Tell me it's not true," he said. His coat was open, almost like he had thrown it on and hadn't bothered to zip it up, and his arms were folded across his broad chest. His dark hair, always a little too long, was mussed up, like he had just gotten out of bed and thrown on the Packer sweatshirt and jeans he had on.

"And a good morning to you, too," I said. "Would you like to come in? I've got coffee and a freshly baked coffee cake."

He closed his dark eyes briefly. "I can't believe it. No, I take that back. I *can* believe it."

"Is that a yes on the coffee cake?"

He glared at me as he stepped inside. "Don't think you can bribe me with baked goods."

"I wouldn't dream of it," I said, closing the door behind him and heading to the kitchen to get out the plates and cups.

He arrived a few minutes later, coat off, and looking even less happy than before, if that was even possible. "Charlie, I swear, sometimes I think you really have a death wish."

I handed him his coffee and gestured toward the table. "The coffee cake is still warm, so it should be good. I was just about to start the bacon and egg casserole, if you want to stick around a little longer."

"Stop trying to change the subject," Wyle said as he sat down next to me. "Why, oh why would you bring home a complete stranger and let him stay in your house?"

"He's Santa," I said, pushing the coffee cake toward Wyle. "He's not a complete stranger."

"That's even worse," Wyle said, glaring at the coffee cake before helping himself to a slice. "He's a delusional stranger."

"He's a harmless old man who needs help," I said.

"You don't know if he's harmless or not."

"I do know he needs help," I said. "He's clearly confused and needs someone to help him out while he regains his memory."

"That may be true, but it doesn't have to be you," Wyle said, taking a bite of the coffee cake.

"But who else would it be?" I asked. "Pat can't."

"Why can't Pat?"

"Well, Richard probably wouldn't allow it," I admitted.

Wyle gave me a pointed look. "Are you hearing yourself?"

"Look, it's only for a few days," I said. "He just needs a place to rest and heal. He might even be better today."

Wyle shot me a look. "Might. He also might be stealing you blind right now."

"I doubt he's stealing me blind," I said. "For one thing, it's not like there's a lot upstairs for him to take. My clothes? My custom teas?"

Wyle closed his eyes again, although I got the feeling what he really wanted to do was bang his head against the wall. "Charlie. You are a single woman living in a house with no close neighbors. It is not safe for you to be bringing home strangers to stay with you, even if you think they're harmless. One of these days, you're going to bring the wrong person home, and it's probably not going to end well."

"I don't bring home just anyone," I said. "I know the risks. I'm careful."

"How can you say that?" Wyle asked, his voice exasperated. "You brought this guy home, and you have no idea who he is. On top of that, he thinks he's Santa Claus. How is that possibly being careful?"

"I told you, he's an old man with health issues. How can he possibly be that much of a risk…" I paused as it suddenly occurred to me that Wyle was in my kitchen wearing a Packer sweatshirt. Wyle rarely showed up at my doorstep to yell at me for getting myself involved in cases in his regular clothes, as he was usually working. "How did you find out that I had Santa here?"

He suddenly became very busy helping himself to another piece of coffee cake. "You know Redemption. It's a small town. And it's not every day Santa shows up, so, of course, people are going to talk."

"That's not answering the question," I said.

"Someone needs to find out who this guy is and where he came from," Wyle said.

"I agree. So are you here on official police business then?"

He frowned at his plate. "Sort of."

"Sort of?"

He let out a sigh. "Today was supposed to be my day off, but I was called in because the storm got us so backed up. I'm going into work in a couple of hours, so I thought I'd swing by here first and make sure you're okay." He met my eyes, and I suddenly forgot what I was going to say.

"Well, hello there." Santa strolled into the kitchen, looking rested, clean, and full of life. Both Wyle and I jumped apart, even though we hadn't been doing anything. We hadn't even been that close.

Santa didn't appear to have noticed. His beard and hair were white and fluffy, like he had washed them, but I didn't remember hearing the shower run. He was back in the same outfit he was wearing yesterday, but I had laundered it last night, so it looked fresh and new. Between his red suit, sparking eyes and bright red cheeks, it was uncanny how much he looked like Santa. "And good morning to you too, Midnight," he said to the cat, who had jumped off his chair at the sound of Santa's voice and went over to rub himself against his legs. "I know you've been a very good cat, haven't you?" Santa said, reaching down to pet him.

"Midnight is usually not that friendly," I said, trying not to look as shocked as I felt. Midnight never acted like that with anyone, not even me. "Especially when he just meets someone."

"Oh, we're old friends, aren't we, Midnight," Santa said, stroking his ears.

"You've met my cat?" I wondered if I had heard him correctly. "When did that happen? When Helen lived here?" Midnight had initially belonged to Helen Blackstone, the previous owner. She hadn't been able to take him with her as she was moving into an assisted living home that didn't accept cats, so she had left him with me. Helen was also a recluse, so while it wasn't entirely out of the realm of possibility that Midnight had met Santa through Helen, it seemed unlikely.

I was also starting to wonder just how many people (or pets) Santa was going to claim to have "met" before.

"Oh, I can't keep track. When you get to be my age, the years blend together," Santa said vaguely, straightening up as Midnight went back to his seat. "I figured you'd be coming by today, Wyle, although I did think it might be a little later. Closer to when Charlie would have her breakfast casserole made."

Wyle looked as taken aback as I felt. "Wait, how did you know my name?"

"And how did you know I was making a breakfast casserole?" I asked.

"Well, I must have overheard, mustn't I?" He winked at both of us and then paused to sniff the air. "Charlie, are your cookies burning?"

I gasped, jumping out of my chair so fast I knocked it over. "Oh no! I forgot." I ran to the oven and flung it open, waving the smoke away and searching for my oven mitts.

"I think they'll probably be fine," Santa said, as I grabbed a dishtowel and carefully pulled the cookie tray out and dropped it with a clatter on top of the stove.

"I don't know," I said, as I bent over to examine them, but other than being a little over-browned on the edges, they did look fine. "Actually, I think you're right."

"Of course I'm right; I'm Santa," Santa said, and let out a deep "ho ho ho" laugh.

I eyed Wyle, who had a befuddled look on his face. I had never known Wyle to be at a loss for words, but it appeared in that moment, that was exactly what had happened. "Can I get you coffee or tea, Santa?" I asked.

"I don't suppose you have a nice cup of milk?" Santa asked hopefully.

Of course he wants milk, I thought as I fetched a glass. He's Santa. "Yep, I'll get it for you if you want to get started on the coffee cake before Wyle eats it all."

Santa chuckled and sat next to Wyle, who still seemed flummoxed. "Have you found my sleigh yet?" he asked Wyle.

Wyle stared at him. "Sleigh? I thought you were in a car accident."

"My sleigh is the one that's missing," Santa said. "Along with my French hens. I don't suppose you found those?"

"Um…" Wyle said.

"And Dremel," I said, handing Santa his milk and taking a seat at the table.

"Oh yes, it would be good to know where Dremel is. Although if anyone can take care of himself, it's Dremel," Santa said, sliding a piece of coffee cake onto his plate.

Wyle's expression looked like he had bit into a lemon. "And Dremel is…"

"My head elf," Santa said matter-of-factly. He scooped up a bite of coffee cake and popped it into his mouth. "He's probably with the French hens, but still, it would be good to know where all of them are."

Wyle's mouth worked, as if he wanted to spit out that piece of lemon, before feeling around for his notebook that was in the back pocket of his jeans. "Can you start from the beginning?"

Santa leaned back, a genial smile on his face. "You were always such a good boy, Brandon."

Wyle's jaw went slack. "I'm sorry?"

"A little on the quiet side but always very observant," Santa said.

"You don't say?" I said, reaching for my own piece of coffee cake and trying not to laugh at the horrified expression on Wyle's face.

Santa nodded. "He was. And a great defender of the downtrodden. I'm not at all surprised he's in law and order, although I did think he would become a public defender."

"A public defender?" I looked at Wyle, whose mouth was still hanging open. "You were going to be a lawyer?"

Wyle looked like he was a fish out of water, gasping for oxygen. "I wasn't … it was just a notion I had in high school until I realized how much schooling was involved if I wanted to be a lawyer."

Santa shook his head sadly. "Such a pity."

Wyle was finally able to close his mouth. "How did you know that?" he demanded.

Santa took another bite of the coffee cake and winked at him. "Lucky guess."

Wyle's eyes bugged out. "Lucky guess? Who guesses that?"

Santa shrugged. "I've always had a knack. Long as I can remember. And besides, you kind of look like a lawyer. Doesn't he, Charlie?" Santa turned to me with a wink.

I looked Wyle up and down with his Packer sweatshirt, disheveled hair, and annoyed expression. Even though a part of me was also wondering how Santa knew that about Wyle, I also found myself enjoying (maybe a little more than I should) Wyle's irritation. It wasn't often that someone got under Wyle's skin the way Santa had managed. "Yeah, he kind of does have that lawyer look."

Wyle stood up, so fast that his chair tipped over. "Charlie, a word?" His voice was strangled, as if he was forcing the words out through gritted teeth.

"Don't mind me, I'm starving," Santa said cheerfully, helping himself to another piece of coffee cake, as I stood up and followed Wyle into the living room.

He grabbed my arm to propel me closer to the door. "Charlie, you have to get rid of him," he hissed into my ear, his voice low.

"What are you talking about? Why?"

"Keep your voice down," he muttered, jerking me even closer. I could smell his soap and shampoo, faint but still there, along with that uniquely male scent that was all him. "He's dangerous." His breath was hot on my ear.

"Dangerous?" Despite my own misgivings, describing the plump elderly man currently munching on coffee cake and drinking milk in my kitchen as dangerous sounded absurd. "How is he dangerous? Because he made a lucky guess that you wanted to be a lawyer?"

Wyle glanced toward the kitchen, as if checking to see if Santa was lurking in the doorway. "Just like it was a lucky guess that he knew your cookies were burning?"

"He could probably smell those."

"And that you were going to make a breakfast casserole?"

"It must have been like he said. He overheard us talking in the kitchen. It wasn't like we were trying to be very quiet," I said, even as an uneasy feeling settled in my gut. Santa did have a knack of mysteriously knowing a lot of things he had no business knowing.

Wyle tilted his head, a knowing expression on his face. "What other 'lucky guesses' did he make?"

I swallowed hard. "It wasn't anything really. He knew Tiki's name…"

"Tiki? You mean Pat's dog?"

"Yes, but Pat or I must have said her name," I said quickly, even though I was pretty sure we hadn't.

Wyle didn't look convinced. "He knew the name of Pat's dog? Like how he knew Midnight?"

"Not exactly," I said, trying to ignore the sinking feeling in my stomach that was getting stronger and stronger. How did Santa know all of these little details anyway? One or two could be explained away as some sort of weird coincidence, but now that they were starting to pile up, it was getting more and more difficult to keep believing there was a perfectly reasonable and innocent explanation for all of it—although I still felt it was over the top to characterize the jolly old guy, who I could now hear chatting to my cat, as dangerous. "It must have been like he said—he met Midnight back when he was Helen's cat."

Wyle shot me a look. "Yeah, I'm sure that's exactly what happened. One day Santa showed up on Helen's doorstep, and she invited him in for a cup of tea and to meet Midnight. Maybe she gave him a tour of the house while she was at it."

When Wyle put it that way, it sounded even more unlikely, but I wasn't ready to admit it yet. "I barely met the woman, and you never met her at all, so I'm not going to presume to know what her actions may or may not have been."

"She was a well-known recluse," Wyle said.

I threw up my hands. "Fine. How do you explain what's going on?"

Wyle's eyes flickered toward the kitchen again. "I can't. Not yet anyway. But it feels to me like he's some sort of con artist, and he's setting you up for the long game."

My mouth dropped open again. "Con artist? What would he be conning me out of?"

"Your trust fund, for one," Wyle said.

"My trust fund. How would he even know about my trust fund?" I was originally from New York, and my family was quite wealthy, hence why I had a trust fund. But it wasn't enough for me to live on for the rest of my life without some supplementing, which was where my tea business came in. My trust fund covered the mortgage and taxes while my business took care of the rest of my expenses.

"If he did enough research to know the name of your cat, he would know about your trust fund."

"But, that's silly. How would he possibly be able to get his hands on my trust fund by pretending to be Santa. Santa leaves you gifts, he doesn't take them."

"That's why it's called the long con," Wyle said. "First, they gain your trust, and then something happens, so they need money. Maybe Santa is going to tell you that he was on his way to deliver thousands of presents to needy children across the country, but instead, he was in a car accident and all the presents were stolen. Now he needs money to replace them, which is where you come in."

"That would be a heartbreaking story, but I also wouldn't turn over my trust fund for that," I said.

"They may not need you to turn over your trust fund," Wyle said. "He may just need to find the information about your trust fund, and he'll use that to drain it."

"He'd have to go through Mr. Farley first," I said. Mr. Farley was in charge of my trust, which meant any withdrawals had to be approved by him personally. He took his job very seriously, and I didn't think he would be at all amused at Santa showing up with a story about presents and needy kids.

"You'd be surprised what a good con artist can do," Wyle said darkly.

"While I'm sure that's true, I don't think that's what this is," I said.

Wyle gave me an exasperated look. "Then what do you think is going on?"

"I haven't a clue, but to me, it feels like if that man is a con artist, and this is all one big con, he wouldn't have chosen a fictional character to pretend to be."

"Why not?"

"Because it's too obvious," I said. "Everyone knows Santa doesn't exist, so why on earth would you pick a character that doesn't exist? That's like pretending to be a fairy or an alien or something. No one is going to believe you, and they're going to have their guard up, which is going to make it more difficult to fall for a con. Wouldn't it make more sense to pick something that was a little less … pretentious?"

Wyle frowned, but I could see the wheels turning. "Well, what else could it be? We know he's not Santa, so there's got to be something else going on, something we're missing."

"Oh, I disagree," Santa said from where he stood just a few feet away from us.

Both Wyle and I jerked our heads over in surprise. Neither one of us had heard him come into the living room. For a big man, he could move very quietly. "How did you get there?" Wyle demanded.

"What do you mean? I walked in," Santa said, gesturing toward the kitchen. "I wasn't trying to overhear, but you just kept getting louder and louder."

Wyle and I glanced uneasily at each other. I was sure we had kept our voices low. Santa must have exceptional hearing.

"But, I digress," Santa said. "There *is* another explanation to everything you've witnessed."

"What's that?" Wyle asked warily.

Santa beamed at us, spreading his hands out. "Why, that I'm Santa, of course."

Chapter 4

Wyle closed his eyes. "Oh, for Pete's sake. I should have known that was coming."

"Think about it," Santa said, ticking things off with his fingers. "If I was Santa, I would know who you are. I know who everyone in the whole world is, along with their wonderful little pet companions, like Midnight and Tiki, bless their sweet little hearts."

An answering meow floated in from the kitchen, and Santa chuckled.

Wyle looked between the kitchen and Santa, then decided to ignore the cat altogether. "That's impossible, you can't know who everyone is."

Santa gave him an amused look. "It's not impossible for Santa. How else am I supposed to deliver all of those presents in one night?"

"Because you don't," Wyle said. "This is a ridiculous conversation. Everyone knows there is no such thing as Santa."

Santa smiled indulgently. "If you say so."

Wyle pressed his lips together in a flat line. "I don't have time for this. I have to change and get to work." He looked at me. "Are you going to be okay?"

"I'll be fine," I said. "Besides, I still have a breakfast casserole to make."

"That's absolutely right," Santa said.

Wyle was still looking at me, his expression torn. I knew he probably did need to get to work, but he also didn't want to leave me alone with Santa.

"It's going to be fine," I said, not sure if I was reassuring myself or Wyle. While I still didn't believe Santa was any sort of a threat, it was still a little concerning how much Santa knew about us. Had we been targeted somehow? And why us?

"We've got plenty of things to do," Santa said and winked at me.

"That's true," I said, as it suddenly occurred to me, I knew exactly what I needed to do, and I couldn't believe I hadn't thought of it before. "And we're going to start by looking for your sleigh, right Santa?"

"And the French hens," Santa said. "If Dremel hasn't found them yet, they're probably pretty hungry and cold."

Glancing outside at the beautiful and frozen winter wonderland, I mentally crossed my fingers that Dremel had found the birds. I didn't have a good feeling that they would have survived the night if they weren't used to Wisconsin winters.

There was a quick knock at the door before it opened. "Good morning," Pat sang out. She was carrying Tiki, who was wagging her tail eagerly. Today Pat had dressed her in a red Santa sweater with matching red ribbons. "How did everyone sleep?"

"Like a baby," Santa said and waved at Tiki.

Pat looked him up and down. "You do look much better. Do you have your memory back?"

"No, I still don't remember anything after Dremel yelled 'watch out,'" Santa said sadly.

"I see," Pat said neutrally, eying me.

"We're going to be looking for a sleigh after breakfast," I said.

"Along with the French hens," Santa said.

"Ah," Pat said.

"I've got to go," Wyle said as he moved to get his coat, his expression more relieved now that Pat had arrived. "Let me know if you find anything."

"Will do," I said.

Wyle nodded at me, shooting one last hard look at Santa before heading out the door.

As soon as the front door was shut, Santa clapped his hands together. "So, about breakfast."

* * *

"If you're really Santa," Pat said as she twirled her fork. We had just finished breakfast and were sitting at the table with empty plates in front of us. "Then how do you deliver all those toys in one night?"

"Now, now, now," Santa said. "That's a trade secret. You can't expect me to reveal a trade secret. They might take my Santa license away from me."

"Horrors," I said. "All those kids might not get their presents."

"Exactly," he said, nodding solemnly.

"So, what do you say to all of those people who don't think you exist?" Pat asked.

"Why do I have to say anything to them?" Santa asked. "It's not my job to convince them of anything. People believe wrong things all the time, that's just the way it is. It's nothing to get all worked up about."

"That's a good point," I said. "But, what about all the parents who are buying presents for their kids, wrapping them, and putting them under the tree? They would say there aren't any presents under there that didn't come from them."

Santa flashed a small, secret smile. "It's not always obvious what my presents are."

Pat and I both waited for him to say more, but he simply sat there, smiling at both of us.

"Well," Pat finally said. "I think it might be easier to believe in you if there was more … evidence you existed."

"There's plenty of evidence," Santa said. "People just need to know how to look."

It was all I could do not to roll my eyes. Pat glanced at me, and I could see she had the same thought. "With all of these riddles, you probably are Santa," I said. "It would be nice if you could give us a straight answer."

Santa let out one of his long belly laughs. "Where's the fun in that? Besides, isn't that what life is? It's not like you get an instruction manual when you're born. Everything is a riddle. You just need to do your best to find the right answers for yourself."

"Are you Santa or a personal development guru?" Pat asked drily, causing Santa to laugh a second time.

There was a loud knock at the front door, followed by the doorbell ringing.

"My goodness," Pat said as I got up to answer. "Who could that be? Talk about impatient."

Santa's face brightened. "Maybe it's news on my French hens!"

"We can only hope," I said, making my way to the door. Whoever was on the other side of it had gone back to pounding on the door. "Hold your horses, I'm coming," I yelled as I reached the door. I didn't even bother looking in the peephole, instead just flinging it open.

Wyle was on the other side, this time dressed in his cop uniform, but his hair was still disheveled, and his eyes were a bit wild. "Is he still here?"

I blinked at him. "Do you mean Santa?"

Wyle looked like it was all he could do to not push past me. "Who do you think I'm talking about?"

"Well, of course, he's here, we've barely finished breakfast…" I started to say, but Wyle didn't let me finish as he strode past me and headed to the kitchen.

"Hello again, Brandon," Santa said, beaming at him. "Does this mean you found my French hens?"

Wyle leaned over the table toward Santa. "Enough of this. Who are you? Really?" His eyes glittered.

Santa appeared unruffled. "I told you. I'm Santa Claus."

"Do you have ID?"

"Why would I need ID?"

"Because that's how you survive in today's society," Wyle said. He kept his tone neutral, but I could see a muscle twitching in his jaw.

"Maybe for other people," Santa said. "But I'm doing just fine. Wouldn't you say?" He smiled at Wyle, whose expression didn't change.

"If you don't show me any ID, I'm going to have to bring you down to the station. Is that what you want?"

"Not particularly, but you need to do what you need to do," Santa said, still appearing completely unruffled. "I can't show you what I don't have."

"Why would you have to bring him down to the station?" I asked. "I didn't think it was against the law to not have ID."

Wyle's eyes flickered toward me, his expression black. "Murder is most definitely against the law." His voice was flat.

I gasped. "*Murder*?"

"How did we get from not showing your identification to murder?" Pat asked.

Wyle shifted his glare to Pat. "Will both of you just stop? I'm trying to do a job here."

"And he's doing a fine job," Santa said. "I always knew you'd make a great cop. Well, truth be told, I did think you would end up a lawyer, but that's beside the point. I knew you'd be good at whatever you set your mind too."

Wyle went back to glowering at Santa. "Are you going to tell me who you really are, or do we need to chat about it down at the station?"

"Wyle, just hold on a second," I said, still trying to get my head around what was happening. "What is this about murder?"

"And what does it have to do with Santa?" Pat asked.

Wyle straightened, folding his arms across his chest and fixing all of us with a steely look. "We found a body."

"A body? Whose?" I asked.

"Not the French hens I hope," Santa said.

I got the impression Wyle was trying hard not to roll his eyes. "No, not French hens. It's a man."

"A man?" I couldn't believe what I was hearing. "You find a body somewhere and just like that, decide Santa must have had something to do with it?"

Wyle's eyes were like chips of ice as he stared at me, making me shiver. I folded my own arms across my chest, mostly for warmth. "He was found in the vicinity of where you picked up Santa."

I lifted my chin defiantly, even though I was starting to get an uncomfortable feeling in my gut. "That could be coincidence. It was a busy street, and the weather was dreadful. People do die during snowstorms."

Wyle's eyes narrowed. "I don't believe in coincidences."

"That doesn't mean they don't exist."

"It does seem like a bit of a stretch," Pat interjected, glancing uneasily between us. "I'm sure lots of people drove by that area the past few days. Are you talking to all of them?"

Wyle shot Pat a look. "He also didn't have an ID."

"Again, not a crime," I said, as the uncomfortable feeling grew stronger. "Just because both Santa and this man didn't have ID doesn't mean they have anything to do with each other."

A muscle jumped in Wyle's jaw. "He was wearing an elf suit."

Silence. We all turned to look at Santa, who was looking disconcerted. "Was his hair blond or red?"

Wyle stared at him. "Red."

Santa sighed. "Oh, dear."

"So you do know him?" I asked.

He nodded. "I think that's probably Drexel."

"Drexel? You mean Dremel?" I asked.

He shook his head sadly. "No, it's Drexel."

"What's Drexel's last name?" Wyle asked. "Or is Drexel his last name?"

Santa blinked confusedly. "His name is Drexel."

Wyle closed his eyes. I could almost see him counting to ten in his head. "Who is Drexel?"

"He's an elf, of course," Santa said.

Wyle looked like he was trying very hard not to throttle Santa.

"How did Drexel die?" I asked, thinking if someone didn't do something, Wyle was going to arrest Santa just to shut him up. And maybe arrest Pat and I too, just because. "Did it look like it was from the same car accident Santa was in?"

"Not unless the car was actually a gun," Wyle said. "Drexel was shot."

"He was *shot*?" Uh-oh. This wasn't good. No wonder Wyle had stormed in here ready for battle.

"I told you it was a murder," Wyle said. "What did you think I meant?"

"Well, not that," I said. "I guess … well, I don't know what I was thinking." That wasn't entirely true. I actually had been thinking that Wyle was probably—hopefully—exaggerating, but with the mood Wyle was in, I wasn't sure how he would take that.

"So," Wyle said, turning back to Santa. "What can you tell me about Drexel?"

Santa sighed again. "Poor Drexel. He was a very naughty elf."

Chapter 5

"So, why did you call Drexel a naughty elf?" Wyle asked. We were sitting in the police station in one of the interrogation rooms. Wyle had finally had enough and told Santa he was bringing him in for more questions, and of course, Pat and I weren't going to be left home. Even Tiki was here, sitting on Pat's lap looking very festive and Christmasy.

Santa frowned. "Well, he's certainly not very nice to the French hens."

Wyle tapped his pen on his notebook. "Is that all?"

Santa looked surprised. "Isn't that enough?"

"I guess that depends on what exactly he did to the French hens," Wyle said drily.

Santa looked thoughtful. "True. I hadn't thought of it that way."

Even though none of this was any of my business—Wyle had made it very clear I was simply here as an observer, nothing more—I felt like this was getting off track. "Why did you have Drexel working for you if he was naughty?"

Santa eyed me over his glasses. "Drexel didn't work for me. I don't have naughty elves working for me." He seemed put out I would even suggest such a thing.

"Wait a minute," Wyle interjected. "Drexel wasn't with you?"

Santa shook his head. "Of course not. I fired him."

Wyle stared at him. "You *fired* him?"

Santa cocked his head. "Wouldn't you?"

Wyle still looked floored. "When did you fire him?"

Santa looked up at the ceiling. "Hmm. I can't remember now. The years all blend together."

"Are you saying you fired him years ago?"

"At least that long ago," Santa mused. "Maybe more."

Wyle raked his hand through his hair. "You better start from the beginning. How long have you known Drexel?"

"Oh, I can't remember that long," Santa said. "He worked with me for years. Was excellent at woodworking. Used to make the best rocking horses." He clapped his hands together, a dreamy look on his face. "Oh, they were wonderful. Children raved over those horses."

"So, what happened?" Wyle asked. I noticed he wasn't taking notes, which wasn't normal for him.

"Well, things change. Children aren't as interested in wooden toys anymore. It's really a shame. Now they all want things like Nintendos and toys with batteries that light up and move. So, we didn't need so many woodworking elves anymore. Some of them adapted, but some didn't. Drexel didn't."

"That's why you fired him?" Wyle asked.

"Drexel lost his way. It's quite sad," Santa said.

Wyle studied Santa for a moment, before dropping his pen and sitting back in his chair. "You are really good."

Santa looked confused. "Of course, I'm good. I'm Santa!"

"That's what I mean. You haven't broken character once. Even when Charlie found you on the side of the road in the middle of a blizzard. And you even had a concussion. How do you do it?"

Santa smiled. "I'm just being myself. That's all."

"What I can't figure out," Wyle continued as if Santa hadn't answered. "Is your angle. What's your end game? At first, I thought it was money, because, let's face it, everything is about money. But, now I'm thinking you're trying to get away with murder."

"Oh, poor Drexel," Santa said sadly. "I knew it wasn't going to end well for him. But there was nothing I could do. He wasn't going to listen to me."

Wyle stood up. "Charlie, Pat. Can I see you outside?"

Mystified, we both stood up and followed Wyle into the hall-way. "Take your time," Santa called out as Wyle shut the door.

"This has gone on far enough," Wyle said. "We have to get an actual name from him."

"Well, can't you do something?" I asked. "You're the profes-sionals, as you keep saying."

Wyle's mouth worked like he had tasted something bad. "We're doing what we can, but so far, we're not getting any-where."

"He's not in the system?" Pat asked.

"No, but that's not that unusual," Wyle said. "If he's never committed a crime before, we wouldn't have a criminal record. But, we're expanding our search, just to make sure."

"What are you going to do if you can't figure out his identity?" I asked.

"Well, what I want to do is get him evaluated by a psychiatrist."

"A psychiatrist? You think Santa is crazy?" Although even as the words left my mouth, I realized how ridiculous they sounded. Of course he would think Santa was crazy. Any sane person would think someone who thought they were Santa was crazy.

"I actually don't think he's crazy," Wyle said. For a moment, I thought he was being sarcastic, but then I realized he was being serious. "I think this is all an act, and a good one. I wasn't kidding in there when I said he was good. However, on the off chance it isn't an act and he is delusional, I want him evaluated. Also, it's possible that the psychiatrist may be able to uncover some clues to help reveal his identity. But, right now, it's a moot point, unless I can figure out how he's involved with this murder."

I held up a hand. "Wait a minute. You're assuming Santa is a murderer?"

"Don't you? It makes the most sense," Wyle said. "He's doing this whole Santa act so everyone assumes he's innocent. Santa wouldn't kill anyone, after all. It's brilliant."

"Yes, but you just said the victim was dressed like an elf," I said. "That sounds like the elf was a part of this as well."

"I know, that's the connection I need to figure out." Wyle's expression was pensive, as if he was struggling to put the pieces together.

"I honestly don't think Santa had anything to do with Drexel's death," I said. "I agree that if this is an act, it's a good one, but murder? I'm not feeling it."

"Maybe he's pretending to be Santa to spread more Christmas cheer," Pat suggested.

"Oh, now there's an idea," I said.

"Oh, come on," Wyle said. "Don't be absurd."

"Why is that absurd?" I asked. "Why do you have to assume he's pretending to be Santa only for nefarious reasons, like he's trying to con someone out of money or get away with murder?"

"That's absurd because it's not how human nature works," Wyle said. "He's not going to go through all of that trouble just for spreading Christmas cheer."

"How do you know?" I asked. "Maybe this is his way of doing some good in the world."

"Maybe," Wyle said, his voice skeptical. "I would have been more likely to believe that before a body showed up."

"Yes, the body of his elf is troubling," Pat said.

"So, why did you bring us out here?" I asked. "Just to tell us that now you think Santa is a murderer?"

"That, and…" He paused, and he looked away. "I need your help."

"What was that?" I asked, before glancing at Pat. "Did you hear something?"

"The only thing I thought I heard was the sound of ice crystals forming in hell, but that couldn't be right," Pat said.

Wyle glared at both of us. "Ha, ha. You two are funny."

Pat grinned. "We'll be here all week."

Wyle's expression grew more serious. "Seriously. I need your help."

"I'll bite. What do you need help with?" I asked.

Wyle looked away and took a deep breath. "I need your help getting to the bottom of whatever is going on."

"Hold on," I turned to Pat. "Did you hear that? I thought only the professionals were supposed to help?"

"Never mind," Wyle said, gritting his teeth and turning away. "I'll find another way."

"No, wait a minute, Wyle," I said, grabbing his arm. I was starting to feel a little bad about teasing him as I did want to help. But only a little. "We didn't mean anything. What can we do?" I gestured toward Pat and myself.

Wyle looked between us, then ran a hand roughly though his

hair, mussing it up even more. "For the record, I'm not happy about having to do this."

"Noted," I said.

"If we weren't so swamped from the storm, it might be a different story, but on top of my normal workload, we have dozens and dozens of claims and traffic accidents and…" He shook his head and raked his hand through his hair.

"Got it," I said. "So, what do you need us to do?"

Wyle took a deep breath and looked at each of us. "Santa trusts you, so I'm hoping you can get him to open up to you. Whatever you can discover would be helpful, but obviously, if you can get a confession, or even his real name, that would be ideal."

"We'll do what we can," I said, glancing at Pat. The confession part didn't seem likely as I still wasn't convinced Santa had killed anyone, but I didn't think it would be productive to keep arguing with Wyle about it. "But first, I have a few questions."

"Of course you do," Wyle sighed.

I put my hands on my hips. "How can I help you if I don't have all the answers?"

Wyle shot me a look. "You and I both know that's not what's going on, but fine. Fire away. I'll answer what I can."

I wanted to remind him that he was the one who had asked for my help this time, but I decided not to push him. He might decide to rescind the request after all. "So, Drexel. What exactly happened to him?"

"I told you; he was shot."

I tried not to roll my eyes. "I know that. But what else? Where was he shot? Do you have a time of death? And where did you find his body?"

"I was wondering that too," Pat piped in. "You said you found him close to where we picked up Santa, but I don't remember seeing anything even remotely like a dead body there. It's a busy street, I feel like that would have caused quite a ruckus."

Wyle put his hand up. "Woah. Slow down and give me a chance to answer. First," he ticked it off his hand. "He was shot in the back."

"The back?" That surprised me a little. "Like he was running away?"

Wyle's look was unreadable. "That's what it appears like. We're not sure about the time, the cold messed that up some, but he was found early this morning by a plow operator."

"He was in the street?"

"In an alley," Wyle said.

Pat blinked at him. "Alley? There's no alley where we picked up Santa."

"It was about a block up or so."

I tried to picture where Wyle was talking about. "The one behind Aunt May's?"

"No, next to the Tipsy Cow."

Pat chewed on her bottom lip as she thought about it. "I guess that's … sort of close, although it's more like a couple of blocks away."

Wyle's expression didn't change. He had what I called his cop face on, but I could see the exasperation in his eyes. "It's close enough to where you found Santa. He easily could have shot Drexel, then walked over to where you found him."

"In that storm?" Pat shook her head. "I would be surprised if he could walk ten feet."

"Not to mention he was injured," I said.

"You'd be surprised what people can do if they have to," Wyle said darkly.

"So, let me get this straight," I said. "According to you, in the middle of a snowstorm, Santa shot Drexel in the back, left his body in an alley, then walked two blocks where we would find him. Did he do all of that before or after he got the concussion?"

Wyle still had on his cop face, but I could tell it was becoming more of an effort. "I get that it's a bit of a stretch…"

I arched an eyebrow. "A stretch?"

He continued as if I hadn't said anything. "Which is why I need someone to get through to Santa or whatever his name is and tell us something helpful. Unfortunately, with all the snow, there's not a lot of physical evidence, so at this point, we don't have a lot of options."

"Yeah, I can see that." I chewed my lip, mulling over everything I knew, which wasn't much, and if there was anything there that would help convince Santa to trust us. "Is there anything else you can tell us? Maybe something about Drexel or his body or something."

I was expecting Wyle to say no or maybe mention some small detail that wasn't going to move the needle much, but to my surprise, he dropped his head and started busying himself with his notebook. He was fast, but not fast enough to hide the two red spots that bloomed above his cheekbones.

"Wyle? What aren't you telling us?" I asked suspiciously.

He muttered something unintelligible under his breath before turning back to us. "It's probably nothing."

"What is probably nothing?" Pat asked.

He made a face. "It's just that Drexel is kind of … small."

I looked at Wyle in bewilderment. "Small? Like … petite?"

"I wouldn't say petite," Wyle said. "More like delicate. Fine boned."

"Delicate," I said, wondering if I was hearing this right. "That's what makes him small?"

"Well, he's short, too," Wyle said. "For a grown man, he's not very tall."

"He's short," I said slowly "Like an elf?"

"No!" Wyle said immediately, but his voice was too loud. "No, no, of course not."

"Wow, I wonder if that means Drexel is also an elf," Pat said. "Just like Dremel."

"No! You're not listening," Wyle said. "There's no such thing as elves. How could Drexel be an elf?"

"You just said he was short," I said.

"And delicate," Pat said. "Or was it fine boned?"

Wyle closed his eyes and took a deep breath. "Okay, look. I'm not going to say I understand any of this, but yes, somehow, they found a guy who has physical characteristics that are elf-like. Like I said, this guy is good."

"Or, maybe Drexel looks like an elf because he is an elf," Pat said.

Wyle gave Pat the stink eye. "The only reason why I'm even telling you is so you know how dangerous that man is." Wyle gestured toward the door. "I know he appears to be a kind, elderly gentleman who wouldn't even kill a fly, but that's only because he wants you to think that. The truth is, he's a very smart con artist who allows no detail to slip through the cracks. You need to be very careful dealing with him."

"Understood," I said, stretching out a hand to reach for the doorknob. "Can we take him home now?"

To my surprise, Wyle shifted his body, so he was blocking me. "Absolutely not." He folded his arms across his chest and shot me an unreadable look. "I may be desperate, but I'm not stupid."

"Uh…" I looked at Pat, who looked as puzzled as I felt. "I'm not sure I understand."

Wyle narrowed his eyes. "I'm keeping him here."

"You're arresting him?" I couldn't believe what I was hearing. Normally, Wyle was cautious about accusing people without solid evidence.

"For murder?" Pat asked. "Or not having proper identification?"

Wyle gritted his teeth. "Neither. I'm simply holding him, which I can do for seventy-two hours without charging him. After that, I will have to let him go if I don't have enough evidence, which is why I need you to work fast."

"But…" I was still having trouble getting my head around what Wyle was saying. It was so unlike him. "How are we supposed to get Santa to tell us anything if he's here and we're out there?"

"You can talk to him as much as you want," Wyle said. "But he has to stay here. You can even leave and come back if you want to, but he can't go anywhere."

"I don't understand," I said. "You do realize you're making it more difficult for us to get him to open up if he's in a police station, don't you?"

Wyle's lips twitched in a small smile. "I have great faith in your persuasion powers."

"Yes, but … you're truly making it far more difficult than it needs to be," I said. "Wouldn't it be easier to just let him go?"

"And have you take him back to your house?" Wyle stared at me, his expression like ice.

I shrank back. "Well…"

"That's exactly why I'm keeping him here," Wyle snapped. "You think I'm letting you take home a murderer? You may have lost your mind, but I haven't."

I licked my lips. "I … uh …" I searched my thoughts to come up with an argument that Wyle might find persuasive, but the only thing I could think of was I didn't think Santa was a murderer. I was fairly certain Wyle wouldn't be swayed by that one.

"What if I stayed with Charlie?" Pat piped up.

Wyle swiveled his head toward her. "Oh, and have not one, but two people at risk for being killed? No thanks."

"He's an old man," Pat said. "There's no way he could take us both down."

"Unless he has a gun," Wyle said.

Pat's face fell. "Oh. That's right. Drexel was shot."

"Exactly."

"Richard would never allow it," I said to her, although I appreciated the gesture.

Pat winced slightly, as if imagining Richard's reaction, before nodding.

"Alright, look," Wyle said. "You two are wasting valuable time. Santa stays here. Those are the terms. Take them or leave them."

Pat and I looked at each other before turning back to Wyle. "What if we aren't able to find any evidence in seventy-two hours?"

"Then it's Plan B," Wyle said ominously.

"What's Plan B?" Pat asked, her voice uneasy.

"You don't want to know."

Chapter 6

"Wyle's keeping me here, isn't he?" Santa asked. His hands were resting on his round stomach, and he looked as calm and relaxed as if Wyle was taking him out to dinner rather than not letting him out of a police station for three days.

"Unfortunately," I said. "Although I'm not supposed to say that." Wyle hadn't officially told him he couldn't leave yet, as he was trying to give us a little more time, which was also why we were still in the interrogation room and Wyle was somewhere else, presumably getting himself a cup of coffee.

Santa rocked back and forth, the chair creaking ominously beneath his considerable bulk. "Brandon really is a good boy. If anyone is going to get to the bottom of who killed Drexel, along with finding my French hens, it's Brandon."

"Wyle is definitely a good cop," I agreed. "I know he's stretched a little thin, so he's asked us to help him out with the investigation."

Santa beamed a smile at me. "Of course he has. You're his secret weapon."

I colored slightly. "I wouldn't say that."

"Oh, don't be so modest," Santa chided. "You're the reason why Redemption has finally started to clean up its act." He leaned closer as he lowered his voice to a loud whisper that didn't seem any quieter than his normal voice. "You have no idea how corrupt Redemption was before. Truly."

Pat looked surprised. "I didn't think it was corruption, I just thought it was because Redemption was haunted."

Santa shook his head sadly. "Oh, no. There were many naughty people here. Very naughty." He pressed his lips together in a disapproving frown.

As interesting as this was, I was also conscious of the time ticking by. Wyle made it clear we didn't have a lot before he had to come in and officially start the process. "Speaking of naughty people, do you have any idea why Drexel was in Redemption?"

"Well, I would imagine because he was trying to steal the toys," Santa said.

It was all I could do to keep my expression steady. All I could hear was Wyle's voice in my head: *Maybe Santa is going to tell you that he was on his way to deliver thousands of presents to needy children across the country, but instead he was in a car accident and all the presents were stolen so now he needs money to replace them.*

Was I about to find out that Santa was a con artist after all? "What toys?" I finally managed, once I thought I could keep my voice even.

"The toys for needy children, who else?" Santa said, like this should have been obvious to me.

I closed my eyes briefly, hoping I wasn't going to have to tell Wyle he was right after all. Hopefully, he also wasn't right about Santa being a murderer.

"What toys for needy children?" Pat asked.

Santa waved his hands. "All the needy children. You know all of those toy drives? Well, someone has to make sure there are plenty of toys for the kids."

Pat narrowed her eyes. "People donate those toys."

Santa winked at her. "Some do, sure. But you didn't think all those toys were donated, now did you? And how would anyone know if a few extra toys were slipped into those barrels across the country? It's not like there's any way to track them, is there?"

"I suppose not," Pat said, her expression thoughtful.

"Did Drexel steal any toys?" I asked, crossing my fingers that the answer would be no.

Santa's face darkened, and I could feel my stomach drop. "Drexel was a very naughty elf."

Wonderful. This was just getting better and better. "Do you know how much he stole?"

Santa waved his hand. "That's Dremel's department. Did I mention he's my head elf? He's got lists and charts and graphs and everything else. He's very organized."

"I'm sure he is," I said, trying not to sound as resigned as I felt. Of course the one person who might be able to shed some light on this mess was missing, and I had three days to find him. "So, it sounds like we need to start by finding Dremel. Any ideas where he is?"

"I'm hoping he's with the French hens," Santa said.

It was all I could do to not start banging my head against the plastic table. "I need something a little more concrete. What about your last memory? Where Dremel said 'watch out.' Do you have any idea why he said that?"

"Probably because there was something in front of him," Santa said.

Out of the corner of my eye, I saw Pat pretend to pull a chunk of her hair out. At this rate, it was going to take us three days just to get a usable lead out of Santa. "Any ideas what?"

Santa frowned as he rubbed his temple. "It may have been one of the reindeer," he said at last.

"Of course. A reindeer," Pat said. "How could we have forgotten about the reindeer?"

"Why was a reindeer in the way?" I asked.

Santa rubbed his head again. "It's all so muddled. I think the reindeer were confused, but I don't remember why."

"What about where you were," I said. "Do you remember looking out the window?"

"Of course I look out the window," Santa said. "Lovely scenery here in Redemption. Beautiful trees."

"Any specific beautiful trees you remember seeing?" I asked hopefully, even though I thought it was a long shot.

Santa rubbed his head and smiled at me, but there was a tinge of sadness. "I'm not very helpful, am I?"

"It's okay," I said, even though I wasn't sure if it was okay. Pat and I had nothing tangible to pursue, and any minute, Wyle was going to stick his head in and tell us our seventy-two hours had started. But one look at Santa's forlorn expression and I couldn't be upset with him. "I know you have a head injury, and that can mess with your memory. I'm sure it will come back." Although I was starting to doubt his memory would come back in time to help us figure out what happened.

"You shouldn't push it," Pat said. "Just relax."

"I'll try," Santa said, and his smile was a little more natural. "It's been a stressful holiday season. Nothing has been going right." He shook his head.

"Like what?" Pat asked, but before Santa could answer, the door opened, and Wyle stuck his head in. His expression was grim.

"Game time," he said.

* * *

"So where do we even start?" Pat asked as we stood in the police lobby, bundling up before heading out to my car.

I blew the air out of my lungs as I wound a scarf around my neck. "I'm not sure."

Tiki stood up on her hind legs, tail wagging, as Pat eased her back in her purse and rearranged her little red blanket around her. "It would help if we at least knew where Dremel was."

"Or the French hens," I said.

Pat shook her head sadly as she jammed her hat on her head. "I don't have a good feeling about the French hens."

"Yeah, I don't either," I said, glancing out the door to look at the sparkling white scenery. It was beautiful … and also deadly. In my mind's eye, I pictured Santa stumbling through the snowstorm, head bleeding, slipping and sliding on the icy sidewalks after shooting Drexel.

I couldn't buy it.

But then I started to think about where Drexel's body was found, and an idea started to form.

"What if we're going about this all wrong?" I said.

Pat eyed me as she yanked her gloves on. "What are you talking about? We have nothing to go on, so what are we doing wrong?"

"We're focusing on the wrong person," I said, feeling the excitement start to bubble inside me.

Pat paused and looked at me in confusion. "I don't understand. Who are we supposed to be focusing on?"

"The victim," I said. "Think about it. We're busy focusing on Santa. Which is understandable as he's the one who doesn't remember what happened to him, and he's apparently the prime suspect. But, if we don't think he is the suspect, then where should we start looking?"

"Where the victim was," Pat said, the light starting to dawn in her eyes.

I nodded. "Exactly. Which means we should start retracing his steps."

"Like where was he before he was shot," Pat mused.

"Yes. I'm thinking if he was in the alley near the Tipsy Cow, maybe he stopped there first."

"Worth a shot," Pat said, as she pushed open the front door, blasting us with a gust of cold air. "Maybe he got into a bar fight, and someone wanted revenge."

"Seems more likely than Santa offing him," I said.

Chapter 7

Unfortunately, it ended up being a good idea in theory rather than practice.

"Sorry, no one was in here matching that description," the heavy-set man behind the bar polishing beer mugs told us. He was in his forties, with a receding hairline and a weak chin. Even though it was still early and as far as I could see, only one person was in there, an elderly gentleman nursing a whiskey at the far end of the bar, the air still smelled of beer and cigarette smoke. He eyed Tiki, who was watching from her purse Pat had slung across her body, but didn't comment.

"Are you sure?" I asked, trying to keep the hopelessness out of my voice. If Drexel hadn't been at the Tipsy Cow, then what was I going to do?

The man gave me a look. "I know." His voice was flat. "I was working, and there was no one in here yesterday who I didn't know personally. Whoever you're describing would have stood out like a sore thumb."

Dejectedly, Pat and I left the bar. "Now what?" Pat asked as we pushed open the front door and let the wind whip around us.

I slumped against the door. "I don't know. That was my last good idea."

"Hey." Pat bumped her shoulder on mine, and even Tiki sat up in her purse to give me a little tail wag. "None of that. We just have to get creative."

"You're right," I said glumly, shielding my eyes against the sharp knife that was the wind. I could feel prickles on the back of my neck, which felt like they were coming from someone watching us but was likely just the wind. "So, if I were an elf…"

"A naughty elf," Pat interjected.

"A naughty elf," I corrected myself. "Who had stolen a bunch of presents from Santa, what would I do?"

Pat stamped her feet against the front stoop. "I would probably be driving away as fast as I could."

"True, but what if you found yourself in a snowstorm and didn't know how to drive in the snow?"

Pat raised an eyebrow. "An elf who can't drive in the snow? He lives at the North Pole."

"Yes, but there are also flying reindeer, so why do you need to drive?" I half smiled before getting serious. "But, think about it. Maybe he drove into a ditch or something and couldn't drive. Then what?"

"We should probably ask Wyle for a list of abandoned cars that were in a ditch," Pat said.

"We definitely should, and that may help us find out who Santa really is, but since Drexel supposedly stole the vehicle and the presents, that's not going to help us figure out who killed him." I frowned as I chewed on my lip. "If he did slide into a ditch, and he couldn't find a cop or a tow truck driver to pull him out, where would he go?"

"Well, to a bar, I suppose," Pat said, gesturing behind her to the Tipsy Cow.

"Or maybe a restaurant," I said, and waited for Pat to catch up.

It didn't take her long. "Aunt May's Diner," she said. "Of course. That's just a block away."

"Exactly," I said. "We could practically walk there."

Pat looked alarmed as she flung her hand out to grab my arm. "But we aren't, right? We're driving."

I glanced down the street in the direction of Aunt May's. Even though a part of me wanted to walk it, to experience what Drexel might have experienced the day he died, I also could appreciate Pat's perspective. It was really cold.

"Of course," I said, digging out my keys. "We're driving."

* * *

"How did you know there was an elf in here?" Sue asked, as she started pouring us both coffee without asking. We were standing by the front counter of Aunt May's, a popular coffee shop that was decorated like a 1950s-style diner. As she poured coffee with one hand, she collected the cream and sugar with the other and slid it between us, then slipped Tiki a piece of a leftover biscuit.

"He was here?" I was so shocked I didn't touch my coffee. Pat, on the other hand, was already busy doctoring hers as Tiki eagerly ate her snack.

Sue blew a lock of brown hair out of her eyes. She was an older woman, round like Pat, with a perpetually red face, no matter what the temperature was. She had been a waitress at Aunt May's for years and years, and seemingly knew everyone in Redemption. "Why do you sound so surprised? You just asked if he was here."

"Yeah, but I didn't think he would have been," I said. So much of this felt like a long shot, I was a little surprised it had paid off. Pat pushed the cream and sugar toward me, and automatically, I started doctoring my own coffee.

"Oh, he was," Sue said, putting the coffee pot back and wiping her brow. "As you can imagine, he caused quite a stir with that outfit he had on. The kids were convinced Santa was here early."

"What did he tell them?" Pat asked.

Sue put one hand on her hip. "Nothing good. He was a complete jerk to those kids. Probably scarred them for life."

"Wow," I said, taking a sip of my coffee. Pat nudged me, and I knew exactly what she was thinking. *Santa did say Drexel was a naughty elf.* "That's disappointing."

"You could say that again," Sue said, shaking her head disapprovingly. "Anyway, why are you asking about him?"

"Well, he was killed," I said.

Sue's eyes went wide. "Seriously? When did that happen?"

"We're not sure," I said. "The storm and the cold meant the coroner couldn't pinpoint the time very accurately, so whatever you can tell us would be very helpful."

Sue shot me a look. "Helpful to you or to the cops?"

"Well, both," I acknowledged. "The department is swamped right now, digging itself out of the storm-related accidents, no pun intended. So, Wyle asked us if we wouldn't mind lending a hand and helping him investigate."

A tiny smile touched the corners of Sue's mouth. "He did, huh? Well, if Wyle asked, I guess I better do my civic duty and tell you what I know, which isn't much. He came in maybe a half hour after the storm started getting really bad and asked if he could use our phone. He looked like something the cat would have dragged in, all wet and muddy. I told him normally we wanted people to use the payphone outside, but we could make an exception for a short local call. I was feeling sorry for him as he looked like he might have been in an accident and maybe needed to call the cops or a tow truck or something like that. I assumed he was going to start telling me what happened, but instead he just stood there and glared at me."

"He glared at you?" I asked.

"Yeah, it was really strange," Sue said, picking up a rag and starting to wipe off the counter. "I didn't take it personally because I figured he was having a really bad day, but still. I was sure he was about to start yelling at me, but instead he asked if he could have a table instead. I told him of course, he could sit wherever he wanted. As you can imagine, we weren't that busy, with the storm and all."

"Where did he sit?" I asked.

Sue pointed. "That booth by the front window."

I turned to look at it. It was positioned so not only would you be able to see anyone who came into the diner, but anyone outside who was walking up to the door.

"Did he order anything?" Pat asked.

"A hot chocolate and a piece of pie," Sue said.

"What kind of pie?" Pat asked.

"Mincemeat."

"I guess that's holiday enough," Pat said. "But he should have been eating cookies."

"We don't have any cookies," Sue said. "But I thought that was just Santa who ate cookies and not the elves."

"The Keebler Elves eat cookies," Pat said.

"They make cookies, I don't know if they eat them," I said.

"Of course they eat them," Pat said. "You can't make cookies without eating them. But, with Santa having such a sweet tooth, I'm assuming everyone at the North Pole eats a lot of sugar."

"Well, he definitely liked his desserts," Sue said gravely. "He polished off both the pie and the hot chocolate in like five minutes. I was heading over to ask him if he wanted something else, when suddenly, his whole body seemed to stiffen, and he shot out of his chair. His face was pale, like he had just seen a ghost. I asked him if everything was okay, and he looked at me in surprise, like he had forgotten about me. I was about to repeat my question when he asked me where the restroom was. I pointed him toward it, and he practically ran over there. And that was it."

"What do you mean that was it?" I asked, rubbing the back of my neck. As Sue was speaking, I had started to feel those prickles again, like someone was watching me, but I had glanced behind me a couple of times and hadn't seen anyone.

"He disappeared." Sue blew another chunk of hair out of her face. "I didn't see him again."

"What, you mean he left without paying?" Pat asked.

"That's exactly what I mean," Sue said disgustedly. "By the time I realized he had been in that bathroom for a little too long, I discovered he had disappeared."

I frowned and turned around again to look at the booth, although I really wanted to check again if anyone was watching me. I kept telling myself I was being ridiculous, the handful of people in the diner didn't seem to be paying any attention to me. They were either chatting to the other people at their table, or in the case of a single man sitting alone, going through a newspaper.

"That's not very Christmasy," Pat said disapproving.

"It certainly isn't," Sue agreed.

I was still examining the diner. "Did you see anything else? Like did someone come in after he went to the restroom?"

"No, I don't think anyone came in," Sue said, but she sounded hesitant.

I snapped my head around to look at her. "What do you mean you don't think anyone came in?"

Sue looked a little embarrassed. "Well, it's just … now that you say that, there was a bit of a ruckus while he was heading to the restroom. Those kids I was telling you about? The ones the elf snapped at? The family was trying to leave so they were all at the door, and the kids were crying, and the parents were trying to comfort them as they got their coats on. It was a mess." Sue shook her head. "It's possible someone stuck their head in during that commotion and decided it wasn't worth staying. But I honestly don't remember seeing anyone do that. And, besides, the weather was awful outside. Would an upset family at the door truly stop them from coming in? I doubt it."

I doubted it, too, except, in this case, it wouldn't be a person looking for refuge and warmth from the cold weather. It would be someone looking for a specific person, who was no longer sitting at a table. Would that person have still come inside? Or would they have instead circled around to see if there was a back door somewhere?

"I have to get back to work," Sue said, picking up the coffee cup again. "If you have more questions, I'm off at five if you want to come back."

"We might," I said, digging out a few bills to pay for Pat's and my coffee. "Thanks for your help."

"Anytime." She grinned at us before hurrying away.

"Hmm," Pat said, finishing her coffee and putting her cup down with a clatter. "What are you thinking?"

I was still savoring mine, so I didn't answer right away. Although, to be fair, it wasn't just the coffee stopping me from answering, it was also that I wasn't sure what I thought yet. It sure seemed to me that Drexel was running away from someone. The question was who … and if they were the ones who killed him.

"Excuse me," a voice behind us said. I turned and saw it was the man sitting at the table reading a newspaper. "Are you looking for an elf?"

Startled, I took a step back. "How did you know that?"

He gave us a sheepish look. "Sorry, I couldn't help overhearing." He gestured toward his ears, which admittedly were large for his head. "Good hearing." He was probably a little older than me, late thirties, with blond hair that was a little too long. A hunk fell across one blue eye, which he impatiently pushed aside.

"Why are you asking?" Pat asked, her voice suspicious.

He swiped his hair again. "Because I'm looking for him, too."

"Why?" Pat asked again.

The man shifted his weight from one foot to another. "He's a … a friend."

Pat opened her mouth, probably to ask what kind of friend, but then her expression suddenly changed as her mouth fell open. "Oh. Are you … Dremel?"

Chapter 8

The man looked startled. "How did you know?"

I wondered how she knew as well. While the man was on the short side, I wouldn't call him small. Or delicate. But, maybe that wasn't a requirement to be an elf.

"Lucky guess," Pat said, as she reached up to finger her hair. The man stared at her, his expression befuddled. "Your hair," Pat said. "It's blond. Drexel is the redhead."

Dremel's face smoothed out. "Oh, of course. I should have known."

"But you're not wearing your elf outfit," I said.

Dremel looked down at his heavy brown fisherman's sweat-shirt and jeans. "Oh. Yeah. You didn't think we always wore our costumes, did you?" He flashed a grin at me.

"I guess not," I said, although I did wonder why they were wearing their outfits yesterday and not today.

Dremel looked like he had read my mind. "We had an engage-ment the day before and were running late for our next gig, so no one bothered to change. Although," his expression turned rueful. "Clearly at this point, that's not going to matter much, as we appear to be stuck here in Redemption for the time being."

"So, you're not really an elf," Pat said, a tinge of disappoint-ment in her voice.

Dremel burst into laughter. "Of course not. We're a theatrical troupe. Christmas is our busiest time."

Of course. How could I have been such an idiot? It was so obvious. It even explained why Santa thought he really was

Santa. If he was one of those actors who went so deeply into his character, hitting his head may have temporarily created the illusion he really was Santa.

Although, it didn't explain the rest, like how he knew things he shouldn't, but I pushed those thoughts away. One thing at a time.

"So, what happened? You were driving through Redemption and got stuck in the storm?" I asked.

Dremel thrust his hands in his pockets. "Basically. We were following Drexel, but we lost him and ended up crashing into a street lamp."

"Oh, no," I said. "Were you hurt?"

"I'm fine," Dremel said as he rubbed his forehead. "My head is still sore, but not too bad. I must have hit it on something when we crashed, but I don't remember."

"What do you remember?" I asked.

"Not much. I remember we lost control and went flying off the side of the road. The next thing I remember was waking up alone in the car, so I guess I must have lost consciousness at some point. So, now I'm trying to track everyone down."

"You were alone?" Pat looked alarmed. "What about the French hens?"

Dremel looked away. "They flew away."

Pat pressed a hand to her mouth. "That's terrible. Those poor birds. And Santa. He's going to be so upset."

"Where is Santa, by the way?" Dremel asked.

"He's safe," I said quickly before Pat could respond. I wasn't sure if it was wise to be telling people where Santa was until we knew more about what was going on. And Santa was basically safe, although I might be stretching the definition to say someone sitting in the Redemption's police department holding cell was safe.

"That's a relief," Dremel said. "I was worried about him. Just like I was worried about Drexel. Do you know what happened to him?" He glanced between us, his expression hopeful.

Pat and I looked at each other, before looking away. I didn't really want to be the one to tell him his friend was dead, but I didn't see that I had much of a choice. "He's dead."

"What?" Dremel's eyes went wide. "He's … no, it can't be. Are you sure?"

"I'm so sorry," I said.

Dremel bit his lip and looked at the ground, shaking his head. "I can't believe it. Poor Drexel. I know he's been in a bad place for a while now, but I had always hoped he would eventually be able to pull himself out of it. I guess it's too late now."

"It's always so sad when that happens," Pat said.

Dremel blew the air out of his lungs before raising his head. "It is. Thank you. Do you … do you know how he died?"

"He was shot," I said.

Dremel's eyes went wide. "What? He was shot? Do the police know who did it?"

"Not yet," I said. "They're still investigating."

"Do you have any ideas who might want him dead?" Pat asked.

Dremel pondered the question. "Not really. Like I said, he had gotten himself in a bad place. I would imagine there were a lot of people who wanted to kill him, but I wouldn't know any of them personally."

"Why would you say that?" I asked.

Dremel grimaced. "He got involved in a lot of … bad things. Lying. Cheating. Stealing. At least that's what I've heard. If I had to guess, I would say he cheated the wrong person, and it finally caught up with him."

That sounded a lot like what Santa had said, but still there was something about his story that niggled at me. "If he had gotten in such a bad place, why was he still a part of the troupe?"

"He wasn't," Dremel said. "At least not officially. But he was still hanging around causing trouble. We couldn't get rid of him."

"Is that why you were following him?" I asked.

Dremel made a face. "We were following him because he had stolen a bunch of stuff from us, and we wanted to get it back."

Again, that seemed to fit what Santa had told us, but still, something was bothering me. Or maybe it was the prickles on the back of my neck, like we were being watched. Initially, I had thought what I had been sensing was Dremel watching us, but now I didn't know.

"Speaking of the van," Dremel was saying. "Do you know what happened to it?"

"What do you mean?" I asked.

Dremel pushed his hands deeper into his pockets and began rocking back and forth. "Well, you found Drexel, I was just wondering if you found the van as well."

"Not yet," I said. "Do you have a description?"

"There's not much to describe. It's pretty nondescript. Just a plain brown van."

"Santa drove a plain brown van?" Pat asked in surprise. "I assumed whatever vehicle he had would be decked out to the max in Christmas cheer."

"Unfortunately, that wouldn't be practical," Dremel said. "We don't want to draw too much attention to ourselves, otherwise it would be too difficult getting in and out of places."

"I guess that makes sense," I said, rubbing the back of my neck again. This case must really be getting to me. I couldn't remember ever being this convinced that someone was watching me before. "So, you're telling us we need to be looking for a brown van."

"Exactly."

* * *

"You found Dremel," Santa exclaimed. "Oh, what a relief. How is he?"

Pat and I were back at the police station while Dremel was still out searching the streets for the van. It had been Dremel's idea to divide and conquer, with the idea we would meet up later at the Redemption Inn as that was where Dremel was staying, and share what we discovered. While part of me thought Dremel's suggestion was reasonable, another part of me wondered if I should have insisted he join us for Santa's sake. Maybe Santa seeing or talking to Dremel would jolt his memory, but even if it didn't, Dremel might know something that might prove Santa's innocence.

It seemed like a no-brainer to bring Dremel to the police station.

So, why was I so reluctant? Why didn't I want to tell Dremel the truth of what was going on with Santa?

I couldn't put my finger on it, just like I couldn't put my finger on why this whole situation was making me so uncomfortable.

Was it just because I thought we were being watched? That was bad enough, especially if Drexel's killer was still lurking around, it was possible we were all in danger, including

Dremel.

Or was it something else?

I could only hope that Dremel would be careful.

"He seems fine," I said. "He hit his head in the crash and thought he might have lost consciousness, but he's okay now."

"Is the reindeer okay?" Santa asked, his voice anxious. He was sitting on a straight-backed chair that he had positioned next to the bars. I was surprised there was a chair in his cell, as I didn't see one anywhere else. I wondered if Wyle had left it for him. Pat and I didn't have that luxury, and we were both standing next to his cell. There were at least six holding cells, but Santa appeared to be the only one being held at the moment. In fact, it seemed like us three were the only people back there, and our voices sounded strange and echoey, although maybe that was just my imagination running away with me.

"Um…" I wasn't sure how to answer that. "Dremel said you hit a streetlamp."

"Oh. That's good." Santa seemed relieved. Tiki had stretched her neck out, sniffing Santa as she wagged her tail. He smiled and reached out to pet her under the chin.

I eyed Pat. "That's … good?"

"That means we didn't hit the reindeer," Santa explained.

"Oh, yes. That would be good." For a moment I wondered if I should mention that Dremel didn't say a word about a reindeer, but then I decided it didn't matter.

"Although when you see Dremel again, make sure you ask him about the reindeer," Santa said, as if reading my mind. "Just to be sure." He waved a finger. "It's very important."

"I'll ask," I said, although now I was wondering if I should tell

Santa that he wasn't actually Santa, and only played one on stage. But, then I reminded myself there was a ticking clock to try and get to the bottom of what was going on before Wyle moved to Plan B, whatever that was, and decided I didn't want to waste time going down that rabbit hole.

"And the French hens?"

This was the moment I was dreading. "Um … Dremel said they flew away."

Santa stared at me, his expression perplexed. "Dremel said they flew away?"

"Yes. I'm just so sorry," I said, my words coming out in a rush. "It's possible we'll still be able to find them. Especially if they're tame birds, which I'm assuming they are, someone might have found them and are taking care of them."

"We can put the word out," Pat said. "Get an article in the newspaper, maybe even get the local radio stations to cover it. They might even be in someone's shed or garage, and we just need to tell people to keep an eye out for them. We should be able to track them down." Her voice sounded far more con-fident about those birds' chances than I was, but maybe Pat had the right idea. Santa still didn't seem like he had recovered from the accident, and he was sitting in a jail cell for a murder I was sure he didn't commit. Giving him some hope that his birds might still be alive seemed to be the least we could do.

Although based on Santa's expression, he didn't seem all that convinced. "If you think so…" he said.

"I do," Pat said firmly. "It's definitely not time to assume the worst."

"Is there anything more you remember?" I asked. "Anything more about Drexel perhaps?"

Santa sighed. "Poor Drexel. He wasn't always a naughty elf,

you know. He made some bad choices, and that led to him falling into the wrong crowd." He looked toward the dirty cinderblock walls.

"Do you know who this wrong crowd is?" I asked. "Maybe a name?"

But Santa didn't seem to be listening. "He had so much talent. Made such beautiful wooden toys. Especially those rocking horses. Such a shame."

I glanced at Pat, and she gave me a slight nod. It didn't seem like we were going to get anything helpful out of Santa. Maybe next time, we should bring Dremel back here, no matter how reluctant I was feeling.

"We're going to keep looking," I said to Santa. "But, we'll be back."

"Of course you are," Santa said, with one of his beatific smiles. "You're both on the good list!"

"Well, we both try," I said, wondering how good I could possibly be. I had certainly made my share of mistakes, some of them very bad.

He chuckled. "Charlie, Charlie, you were always too hard on yourself. Deep down inside, you're a good girl. Never forget that." His lips twitched up into a smile that didn't reach his eyes. Actually, it was more than that, his eyes had an intenseness to them that seemed to bore right through me, allowing him to see all of my secrets, even the ones I kept hidden away.

Charlie, get it together, I muttered to myself, as I started backing away. I wasn't sure why I was having such a reaction to this case, but I needed to get a grip.

"I'm serious," Santa said as I continued backing toward the door.

"Um ... okay," I mumbled, but that didn't seem adequate.

"Thank you," I added. Pat gave me a strange look, so I decided to just shut my mouth.

"Oh, and don't forget to ask about the reindeer," he called out.

Chapter 9

"A brown van?" Wyle repeated, reaching for his notebook, which was balanced precariously on top of a towering pile of paper and folders that presumably was his desk, although it was difficult to tell. As usual, the place smelled like a bad combination of burnt coffee, sweat, and fear.

"That's what Dremel said Drexel was driving," I said.

"I don't suppose you got a license plate number," Wyle said, somehow retrieving his notebook without toppling the rest of the piles over. I was always in awe at how much of a mess Wyle's desk was, and yet he still magically could locate whatever he needed. Not to mention how his stacks of paper seemed to somehow defy gravity.

"Uh, no," I said. It hadn't occurred to me to ask for a license plate. Wyle raised one eyebrow but didn't comment.

"I'll see what I can dig up," Wyle said. "Although I'll warn you, cars that are abandoned aren't always towed right away."

"I was also wondering about checking the accident reports," I said. "Maybe a brown van was in an accident yesterday."

"I'll check, but that seems a bit more unlikely," Wyle said.

"Why? Someone shot him. Maybe it was because of an accident," Pat said.

Wyle gave her a look. "This is Redemption, Pat. You don't think that would have caused some attention?"

"I'm just saying, there was a lot going on yesterday," Pat said.

"If there was an accident yesterday and we had written up a report, I can guarantee we would have noticed that one of the drivers had been shot," Wyle said.

"Oh, for heaven's sake, I wasn't trying to imply you were that incompetent," Pat said impatiently. "I was assuming the shooting happened after the accident and the police report. Or maybe the drivers didn't call the cops, just had it out right there in the street, and it was only later that someone else called it in."

Wyle didn't look all that convinced, but he dutifully wrote down another note. "Anything else?"

"Well, we met Dremel," I said.

Wyle had been looking at his notebook, but his head shot up at that. "Dremel? Is that another elf?"

"He's the good elf," I said.

"Although he lost the French hens," Pat said.

Wyle was looking between us. "How did he lose the French hens?"

"We're not sure. He said they flew away, so it's possible they're still somewhere in Redemption," I said.

"We have to try to find them," Pat said. "Maybe you can put out a bulletin or something?" She gave him a hopeful look.

"I'm not putting a bulletin out for missing birds," Wyle said, then held up a hand as Pat started to protest. "But, I'll see what else I can do. Okay? Now, back to Dremel. Where is he? Why didn't you bring him to the station with you?"

"He's still looking for the van," I said.

Wyle stared at me. "He's what? You just left him to wander around on his own?"

"We're going to connect later and compare notes," I said.

Wyle looked like he was having trouble comprehending what I was saying. "You're going to compare *notes*? Do you understand he could be a material witness in a murder investigation?"

"We don't know that," I said. "He said he didn't know Drexel was dead."

"Oh, well that makes all the difference then," Wyle said, dropping his pen on the notebook and scrubbing at his face. "A murderer would never lie about something like that."

"Yeah, just like a murderer would never run if he knew the cops considered him a material witness to the crime," I retorted. "Give me some credit. I didn't share much of what was going on with him."

"But you told him Santa was in custody, right?"

"Actually, I didn't," I said. "I didn't know if you wanted that information out there, so I kept it to myself. Which is why when he volunteered to keep searching the streets because he said it made sense for us to split up, I couldn't think of a good reason to bring him in."

Wyle glared at me, his expression shifting around, like he was trying to figure out how to react to what I was saying and couldn't decide which way to go. Finally, he picked up his pen. "What's his name, and where is he staying?"

"Dremel, I told you," I said.

He closed his eyes briefly. "You didn't get a last name?"

"There was no reason to," I said.

"Where is he staying?"

"At the Redemption Inn."

"If it helps," Pat chimed in, "he said he and Santa are a part of a theatrical troupe."

"That might help," Wyle said, jotting that down. "Although I don't suppose you got the name of the troupe." He glanced up at us before sighing. "Of course you didn't."

"There was no reason to," Pat explained.

"Of course there wasn't." He eyed us both. "Was there a reason to ask if he and Santa were in an accident?"

"Actually, that did come up," I said. "Dremel said they were chasing Drexel, who had stolen Santa's van, and Dremel ended up losing control of the car and hitting a streetlamp."

Wyle's eyes widened. "A streetlamp? They crashed into a streetlamp?"

"That's what he said."

"Did he happen to mention where this streetlamp was?"

I glanced at Pat. "Um…"

Wyle pinched his nose. "I know. It didn't come up."

"He's new in town," I said. "So, would he know? And it's not like this was an interrogation. It was just a friendly chat."

"A friendly chat," Wyle said, shaking his head. "What about Santa's real identity? Any updates on what I actually asked you to look into?"

"What are you talking about?" I asked indignantly. "We made a lot of progress."

"Yeah, we found Dremel, and we know that Drexel was driving a brown van," Pat said.

"Oh, and he was also in Aunt May's before he was killed," I said.

Wyle eyed both of us. "You do know we're investigating Drexel's murder, right?"

"But don't you see, it's all connected," I said.

"If it was all connected, why didn't you ask Dremel what Santa's real identity was?" Wyle asked.

Yikes. Good question, not that I wanted to tell him that. "Um…" I said, glancing over at Pat to see if she could help. She looked as chagrined as I felt.

Wyle put a hand up. "Never mind. I don't want to hear the answer. The point is, you're supposed to be focusing on finding out who Santa is, not poking around in a murder investigation."

"We tried," I said. "We talked to Santa, but he didn't know anything, so we got creative." I spread out my hands. "And look at all we learned. Or," I lowered my hands and tilted my head. "Did you already know about Drexel being at Aunt May's?"

"Drinking hot cocoa and eating a piece of pie," Pat added. "Mincemeat."

Wyle looked like he was trying to decide between strangling us and asking more questions. Being a cop won out, and he poised his pen on his notebook. "Tell me everything."

I quickly filled him in on what Sue had told us as he jotted down notes. "So, you think he might have seen someone and that's why he ran out of the diner without paying?" Wyle asked when I finished.

"That or he didn't have any money," Pat said.

"Why would you think he didn't have money?" Wyle asked.

Pat looked at him like it was obvious. "He's an elf. Elves don't have money."

Wyle muttered something under his breath and stood up. "Give me a sec. I'm going to check on a few things."

"He doesn't seem very happy with what we uncovered so far," Pat said as we both watched Wyle stride across the room.

"Well, it's not like he gave us a lot to go on," I said. "We're doing the best we can." Although I was wondering if that was true. I hadn't said anything to either Pat or Wyle about feeling like someone was watching us, nor my uneasy feelings about what we were uncovering, and I wondered if that was a mistake.

He returned in a moment, an unreadable expression on his face. "It appears we may have found your brown van."

"Really?" I was floored. "Where is it?"

"It's in impound."

"Well, let's go," I said, standing up. Pat did the same.

"Oh, no," Wyle said quickly. "You two are staying out of it."

"What are you talking about?" I asked. "We found the lead for you. You can't not let us be a part of it."

"Look, I'll tell you what I can," Wyle said. "But, for right now, you have to let us handle it. Remember this is an active murder investigation, and it would be too difficult to explain why I brought you two with me."

He had a point. As much as I hated to admit it.

"Fine," I grumbled.

He paused and flashed me a faint smile. "I appreciate what you're doing. Truly. So, now it's my turn to go do my job. In the meantime, you two can keep digging around in Santa's past. The sooner you can figure out his actual identity the better."

"We'll do our best," I said as Wyle plucked his jacket that hung from the back of his chair and headed out.

"So now what?" Pat asked, as we both collected our coats.

"Maybe see if we can find Dremel? Maybe he found something." That felt sort of lame, but it was all I could think of. Even if Dremel hadn't found anything, maybe just walking around the streets where Drexel was killed would spark something.

"Might as well," Pat said as we walked through the police station and toward the lobby. "If nothing else, we can ask him about the reindeer."

"That will at least make Santa happy," I said.

As we neared the lobby, I could see there was a ruckus going on. "I need to talk to someone," a familiar voice was insisting although I couldn't quite see who was talking.

"Ma'am," a tired voice answered her. "I promise you, I will have someone contact you as soon as I can."

"Wait," Pat said next to me. "Is that … Mildred?"

"It sure sounds like her," I said, quickening my step. Mildred was one of my elderly tea clients who fancied herself something of an amateur detective. I had helped her last year when she thought her next-door neighbor had hired a vampire as a house sitter. Luckily, we had gotten that sorted out without needing to use wooden stakes or cloves of garlic (Mildred had come prepared.) Ever since, she has been looking for her "next case."

"Mildred," I called out as soon as she came into view. "What are you doing here?"

Mildred looked up from where she was still arguing with the officer sitting behind the desk, and her face broke out into a huge smile. "Charlie! Pat! Why are you here? Do you have another case?" She looked so eager I almost wished I did have something I could use her help with.

Mildred was a retired schoolteacher who now spent her days keeping a close eye on her neighbors and anyone else she thought could use her attention. As always, she was impeccably dressed in black pants and a bright red sweater, and her grey curls looked like they had been freshly permed, although her face was more flushed than usual.

"We're just here helping a friend," I said. Mildred's face fell, and I quickly added, "But what about you?"

"Me? Oh, you're not going to believe what happened to me." Two spots of pink had appeared on her cheekbones. "Someone tried to kill me yesterday."

"Wait, *what*?" I asked.

"Are you okay?" Pat asked.

She pressed a hand against her chest. "I am now. But at the time I thought I was going to have a heart attack."

"Mildred, what happened?" I knew she could be a bit of a busybody, but she was a harmless busybody. I couldn't imagine anyone wanting to kill her.

"Well." She took a deep breath. "It was during the storm. I was driving…"

"Hold on," Pat interrupted. "You were driving during the storm?"

"I had a doctor's appointment," Mildred said. "I had no idea it had gotten so bad until I left the doctor. It was horrible."

"I know; it was horrible," I said. "We got stuck in it, too. So, what happened?"

"It was dreadful," Mildred said. "Slippery and hard to see. And some of the cars were going so fast! Way too fast." She pursed her lips disapprovingly. "I decided to get off the main road and use the side roads. I know they aren't plowed first like the main one, but the way the snow was coming down I didn't think it was going to matter, as the plows didn't seem to be out anyway. So, I made a left on Jefferson. There was another car coming toward me…" She demonstrated with her hands. "And suddenly, it veered out in front of me! Like it was trying to crash into me."

"Oh my gosh, that sounds terrifying," I said. "What did you do?"

"What else could I do? I jerked my wheel to get out of the way and hit a snowdrift."

My eyes went wide. "You hit a snowdrift? And you didn't get stuck?"

"Well, it was more like I slid into the side of the road," Mildred said a little sheepishly. "There was a pile of snow there, though. But I was able to back up and keep going."

"What about the other car?"

"That car got stuck," Mildred said with a sniff. "I don't know what happened exactly, everything happened so fast, but when I was leaving, I could see he was spinning his tires as I left. Good riddance."

I glanced at Pat. This didn't sound like someone had intentionally tried to kill Mildred. "Are you sure he just didn't lose control of his car? It was pretty slippery."

She shook her head. "No, you don't understand. We were both driving slowly, and suddenly, he veered out. It was deliberate."

I was having a hard time believing someone would deliberately swerve into Mildred. "Why do you think he would do that?"

"I don't know! That's why I need the cops to investigate." She turned to glare at the officer behind the desk, who slowly sank down in his seat. Mildred still had that teacher look. "But it gets even worse."

"Worse? How did it get worse?"

"He's still out there."

I tried not to groan. "What do you mean?" I braced myself for hearing a story about seeing him lurking around her home.

But, what she said instead, surprised me. "His car is still there."

"His car is where?"

"On Jefferson. It's still there."

"The car is still there? In the street?"

"Yes. In the exact same place." She folded her arms across her chest. "So why did he abandon his car?"

"Maybe he damaged his car in the storm and couldn't drive it away," Pat said.

"Then he would have gotten it towed," Mildred said. "He wouldn't have just left it."

It was possible the tow truck drivers were just so backlogged they hadn't gotten to it, but I decided not to say that. "Are you sure it's the same car?"

"Of course I'm sure," Mildred said. "You couldn't miss it. It's a brown car. It's big." She started gesturing with her hands.

I stared at her, as an uneasy feeling starting uncurling itself in my stomach. "Are you talking about a ... van?"

Mildred waved her hand. "Van, car, it's all the same. Whatever it was, it almost hit me."

I looked at Pat, whose mouth was hanging open. "Let's go check it out."

Mildred brightened. "Really? You'll investigate?"

"Yes. Let's go."

Chapter 10

"What are the odds it's the van that Drexel was driving?" Pat asked. We were following Mildred as she drove, very carefully and very, very slowly, to Jefferson street.

"I don't know, but how many brown vans could there be in Redemption?" I said.

"At least one, which has been impounded," Pat said. "Are we sure this wasn't the van that was impounded?"

"She said she just saw it. It's got to be a different van."

"Hmm." Pat turned to look out the window. "It's so strange. If it was Drexel, why would he have tried to plow into an old woman?"

"Maybe he didn't realize she was an old woman," I said. "Maybe he thought she was the person he was trying to get away from. The one who ended up killing him."

"That could be," Pat said, as Mildred put on her turn signal. "Isn't Jefferson still a couple of blocks away?"

"Yes," I sighed. "I think she wants to make sure I don't miss it." I looked behind me at the line of cars that was steadily growing longer and hoped none of them were in too much of a hurry.

I saw the van immediately once we turned onto Jefferson Street, although it had been plowed in, so it was covered with snow.

"If it wasn't going anywhere before, now it really isn't," Pat said.

Mildred had pulled over on the other side of the street and was frantically blowing her horn and flipping her turn signal lights off and on. I parked behind her, and Pat and I hurried over to her.

"There's the van," she said. She had unrolled the window half-way and pointed. "See? It's just like I said."

I turned to study the van, buried in snow. "Wait here," I said and raised my eyebrows meaningfully at Pat, who turned duti-fully—and reluctantly—toward the van.

"Even if it is Drexel's van, what are we supposed to do about it?" she asked me, keeping her voice low, although it was cold enough that Mildred had rolled her window back up again. "Maybe we should leave a message for Wyle."

"Before we do that, we probably should at least try to verify if it's Drexel's van or not," I said. "You know Wyle is checking that other brown van out, so we need to be able to give him something more than, 'oh we found another brown van for you to check out.'"

"I suppose," Pat sighed as we continued trudging in deeper and deeper snow. "So, what are we looking for exactly?"

"I'm not sure," I said as I reached the driver's side window. "Maybe something that says 'Drexel was here?'"

"Ha, ha, you're funny," Pat said, rounding the back. I brushed the snow off the window and peered inside. Fast food wrap-pers and empty soda cans littered the floor, and my heart sank. Now what?

"I might have something," Pat said, her voice sounding cau-tiously excited.

"What?"

"Come here. It's hard to explain."

I trudged around the van to find Pat peering in the back win-dow. She saw me and pointed. "Look. Is it what I think it is?"

I waded over to her and looked inside. It was overflowing with … stuff. Stuffed animals, dolls, blocks, toy cars and … Christmas items. Tinsel, ornaments, wrapping paper, bows, even a tree.

I turned to Pat, who was looking more and more excited. "It's got to be Drexel. Don't you think?"

"It does look like a van that a theatrical troupe featuring Santa would be driving around in," I said, trying not to look around as that feeling I was being watched was prickling at the back of my neck again. I had to get a grip. No one would be watching us in the cold and snow, except maybe the owner of the house the van was parked in front of.

"I knew it," Pat said. Tiki popped her head out of her purse and gave her own little yelp.

"I knew you two were special," a voice said behind us. We both turned and saw Dremel standing there.

"Dremel," I said, wanting to kick myself for not turning around sooner. I should have known my prickling feeling was correct. "How did you find us?" The uneasy feeling that had been following me around all day, had started to twist around my stomach again.

"I saw you." He waved haphazardly down the street. "I can't believe you found the van." His voice had a touch of admiration.

I moved a little closer to Pat. "Lucky guess," I said, praying that Mildred would see what was going on and drive away. Better yet, drive back to the police station and ask for Wyle, who I knew would take her seriously even if no one else did, but I thought that might be stretching it.

"That was some lucky guess. I'm impressed." He started walking toward the front of the van.

"Well, every now and then those guesses work out," I said, taking another step closer to Pat, so close we were touching. "So we probably should be calling the cops and letting them know."

Dremel stopped dead, and I immediately knew my instincts had been right all along. Mentally, I started kicking myself for not being more on the ball.

He slowly turned toward us. "Why would you do that? You don't want to waste the cops' time." His voice was agreeable, friendly even, but that just made the uneasy feeling more pronounced.

"Of course not," I said. "But, they already know there's a brown van that's missing. It would be good to close the loop on that, don't you think?"

"I really don't think we should be wasting the cops' time," he said again. Was there an edge to his voice, or was I imagining things?

"I agree. No wasting time," I said. "But, with Santa and all…" I let my words hang.

He stiffened. "Santa? What does he have to do with anything?"

"Well, he's just been … really confused over what happened during the storm," I said. I lowered my voice and made it sound like I was sharing a confidence. "It would help, I think, if we could make him more at ease. He's already upset about the van going missing, and with him facing spending the rest of his life in jail…"

"Santa is looking at jail time?" Dremel interrupted. "For what?"

I looked at him in surprise. "For Drexel's murder, of course. What did you think?"

Dremel turned away but not before I saw his expression rearranging. "Oh. Of course. That makes sense. He was so upset about what Drexel turned into."

I bobbed my head. "I know. It's been terrible. So if we could relieve his mind about the van and the reindeer, I think that would really help."

Dremel's eyebrows furrowed. "Reindeer?"

"Yes, the reindeer. Santa said he remembered the reindeer was what caused the accident, and I think it would make him so much happier if he knew that the reindeer was safe."

Dremel stared at me for a long moment, before finally nodding. "Yes, yes. Of course. That makes total sense. You can tell him the reindeer is fine. Nothing happened to the reindeer."

And just like that, I knew he was lying.

"What a relief," I said, forcing a smile. "He'll be so happy to hear that."

"I'm glad," he said as he started tramping toward the front of the van again. "Now, if you'll excuse me, I have a lot to do."

"What do you mean?" I asked.

He had almost reached the passenger door. "Well, I have to dig the van out, which might take a bit of time, and then hope Drexel didn't damage it so badly that it won't start."

"Don't you think you should wait?"

Dremel glanced at me briefly. "Why should I wait?"

"Because I'm sure the cops are going to want to examine it first. See if there's anything in there that can help solve Drexel's murder."

"I can guarantee there's nothing in here that's going to help the cops out," Dremel said, fumbling around in his pocket, presumably for the key. "However, the show must go on, so the sooner I can get this van on the road, the faster I can get back on schedule."

Despite how the cold seemed to be settling into my bones and all I really wanted to do was get back in my nice warm car, I forced myself to take a step toward Dremel. "I'm afraid I can't let you do that."

He had just fished the key out of his pocket, but he paused at my words, then slowly turned his head. "What did you say?" He didn't sound angry, more like flabbergasted.

I took another step toward him, even though I could hear Pat squeak behind me. Or maybe it was Tiki. "I can't let you do that. The cops need to be notified, and then they need to go through the van. Once it's released, you can take it wherever you want, but first we have to let them process it."

His eyes hadn't left mine, and he slowly tilted his head. "And … how do you plan to stop me?"

Alarm bells started going off in my head. "Do I need a plan to stop you?"

He let out a long sigh. "Oh, Charlie, Charlie," he murmured, before turning to face me, which was when I saw the gun in his hand. "Yes, you absolutely do need a plan to stop me."

Behind me, I could hear Pat gasp. I held my hands out to the side and took an involuntary step back, nearly sliding and falling on my butt. "What are you doing?"

"I thought I was clear." He gestured toward the van. "I'm taking this and leaving."

"But, why the gun?"

"Because you leave me no choice." He waved the gun toward me. "Do you think I wanted to do this? No! All you had to do was let me leave like I wanted, but no. You had to butt in, and now you've made things so messy for me."

"Dremel, you don't have to do this," I said as my mind whirled searching for a way out. Maybe one of the neighbors would happen to look out the window and call the cops. Or … Mildred! Had she left or was she still there, sitting in her car? I couldn't see her because the van was blocking my view, so I had no idea if she was there or not. Oh, I really hoped she wasn't going to get out. Hopefully, instead, she would see what was going on and drive to the police station…

"Charlie?" Mildred's voice called out from the other side of the van, and my heart sank. "What's going on? Did you find something?"

Dremel's eyes went wide. "Who's that?"

"No one," I said, at the same time Mildred yelled "Charlie, who's that?"

"No one," I shouted to Mildred. "Everything is fine. Get back in your car."

"What? I can't hear you," Mildred said, her voice coming toward us. I closed my eyes in despair.

"Mildred, everything is fine," Pat yelled.

"I can't understand you," Mildred said. "I didn't put my hearing aid in this morning."

"You know I'm going to have to kill her, too," Dremel hissed at me.

"Please don't," I said. "She's an old woman. She's harmless."

He brandished the gun at me. "This is all your fault."

"So, what is … oh my heaven's is that a real gun?" Mildred had finally rounded the van and was standing next to Pat.

"Mildred, get back to your car," I said.

"Yes, Mildred, go," Pat said.

"But he has a gun," Mildred said.

"Stop talking! All of you," Dremel yelled, still waving the gun around.

I eyed him, wondering if I would be able to charge him without getting shot. Considering the snow was nearly knee deep, I didn't think I would be able to move quickly enough, just like I wasn't sure if I could run away fast enough. Maybe instead I should be trying to distract him, get his attention on me, so Pat and Mildred could get away. With any luck, they'd get the cops over here soon enough to arrest him.

"Young man, that's very disrespectful," Mildred was saying. "It's bad enough you're pointing a gun at us, but you don't have to be rude about it."

Dremel moved away from the van a few steps to point the gun at Mildred. "I told you to shut up! I need to think."

"Then you should ask nicely," Mildred said. "Use your words. I don't know what they're teaching kids these days. They're so disrespectful."

Dremel gritted his teeth. "I've about had it with you…"

Here was my chance. He was completely focused on Mildred and wouldn't see me coming. Maybe. If I could somehow get up enough speed to run through the snowdrift…

Suddenly, from the other side of the van, there was a blur of motion as three figures rushed Dremel and tackled him. His gun flew through the air, and he disappeared into a mound of snow with limbs going every which way.

"Get the gun," I yelled at Pat, as it had fallen close to where she was standing, and I hurried over as fast as I could to the pile of bodies to try and figure out what was going on. There was a lot of action, as well as a lot of words, which I couldn't understand as they seemed to be in a different language. They also appeared to be said in feminine voices.

"Charlie, is it?" a voice said from behind me, and I whirled around. There was a small, slender figure standing there, who I first thought was a child, but the voice was too low. He wore a bright green stocking cap with a matching bright green jacket, and under his cap, was a shock of blond hair. He made a slight bow. "Dremel, at your service."

"Dremel?" I whipped my head around to the heap of bodies. There was still a steady stream of a foreign language along with the low groans that sounded like they were coming from Dremel. Or, at least who I thought was Dremel. "But that…"

"Is not me," Dremel said, his voice cheerful. "He's the one who killed Drexel, though. So, thank you for helping us find him."

"Who is he then?" I asked.

Dremel shrugged. "I don't know his real name. You'll have to ask him. I just know he killed Drexel."

"If you don't know who he is, how do you know he killed Drexel?" I asked.

He cocked his head. "He held a gun on you, didn't he?"

"Do you surrender?" a heavily accented female voice said.

"Yes, yes, I surrender," the man who I thought was Dremel said meekly.

The three figures hauled him up, and I got a good look at them. They were tall, willowy blondes, also wearing bright green jackets and green stocking hats. "Good," the first woman said. "And don't you forget it."

"Charlie, I'd like to introduce you to April Aguillard, one of our French hens."

"Bon jour," the woman said, bobbing her head.

"Did you say French hens?" Pat asked. She had retrieved the

gun and was holding it away from her body, like it was a snake and she was afraid it might bite her.

"Oui," April said.

"Wait a minute." I turned back to Dremel. "The three French hens are women?"

"Of course they are," Dremel said. "What did you think? They were birds?" The four of them burst into laughter.

I turned to look at Pat, who looked as shocked by the turn of events as I was. "I think I need a drink."

"Who's a French hen?" Mildred asked.

Chapter 11

"Thank you again for taking such good care of Santa for us," Dremel said. The entire lot of them, including Pat and Tiki, were in my kitchen demolishing the cookies I had made. Good thing I had decided to get up and bake this morning.

"We were happy to help," I said. Santa said something to April, who let out a tittering laugh that sounded just like a bird.

As it turned out, the man we thought was Dremel had killed Drexel. His name was Samuel Barrass, and he pretty much confessed the moment the cops arrived. I think the fact the French hens had been sitting on him in the snow helped soften him up.

Apparently, Drexel had a bad gambling problem. He had borrowed money from Samuel, and was having some trouble paying it back. So, in an act of desperation, he had stolen Santa's van full of toys and equipment. He had told Samuel he was going to give him the equipment to sell, and they were supposed to meet at an agreed-upon location where Drexel was going to turn over everything to Samuel. But, Samuel hadn't trusted Drexel, so he had been following him from the moment he stole Santa's van.

But Samuel wasn't the only one following Drexel. Dremel, Santa, and the French hens were as well, and eventually, they had all ended up in Redemption just when the storm was starting to hit.

Drexel managed to elude his pursers, but at the cost of losing control of the van and crashing into the side of the road, after almost hitting Mildred. Dremel also had lost control of his "borrowed" car (it wasn't clear where he had borrowed it from, but maybe it was best not to ask too many questions) when a deer jumped in the road.

"A regular deer, not a reindeer," Dremel said. "I know Santa gets confused at times."

"Well, he did have a concussion," Pat said, although I thought Pat was being a little too generous. Reindeer don't look anything like the white-tailed deer that are so common in Wisconsin.

Also, as it turned out, Samuel had been right—Dremel had hit a streetlight. The car was totaled, and somewhere in the confusion, Santa had wandered away to the spot where we found him.

Samuel had not gotten into an accident, but with the weather so bad, he ended up parking and searching by foot. He spotted Drexel sitting at Aunt May's, but Drexel ran out of the back by the time he reached the entrance. He managed to catch up to Drexel in one of the back alleys. They argued, and Samuel ended up shooting him in the back. He then searched Drexel's body for the key to the van, but by then, the weather was so bad, he decided to hunker down and find a hotel to wait the storm out and then locate the van.

Wyle had no trouble getting the full confession out of Samuel, after he had finished yelling at Pat and me for not telling him about the van.

"You were already looking for a brown van," I told him.

"You still should have said something," Wyle had said. At least he had waited to lecture us until after we were out of the cold and back in the warmth of the police station, although at that point it had turned into a zoo. The French hens were still berating Samuel in French, Dremel was trying to talk his way into seeing Santa, and Samuel just wanted to confess and get it over with.

Wyle was so furious he was practically shaking. Or maybe it was just the cold that was making him shake. "Don't you understand, you could have been killed," he said. "This is why I keep telling you that you have no business investigating and you should be leaving it to the professionals."

"It wasn't ... ideal," I said. "But I couldn't let him leave either."

"Good thing the French hens were there to save the day," Pat said.

"You got that right," I said. As it turned out, we were being watched, but it was Dremel and the French hens who had been keeping an eye on us. They had somehow found out that we were the ones who had picked up Santa, and they wanted to see what we were up to.

Wyle looked like he was going to throttle us both. "And that's the issue. You can't depend on someone else to save you. You need to be smart about things like this. If you had been hurt or killed ..." abruptly he stopped talking and started shaking his head. "One of these days, you're going to get yourself in real trouble."

"I'll be more careful," I said quietly. "I promise."

Wyle looked like he wanted to say more, but instead pressed his lips together and walked away, after muttering something about needing to help process everyone.

After the cops got statements from all of us and released Santa (once Dremel had produced Santa's ID, which did actually say "Kris Kringle" on it, much to Wyle's chagrin) we headed back to my house for some much-needed nourishment. As Pat said, living through a life-or-death situation can certainly whet the appetite.

"Thanks for all the cookies," Dremel continued. "This is exactly what we need before we hit the road again."

"Tonight?" I glanced toward the window and the setting sun. "But it's already getting dark. Don't you want to wait until morning?"

"Oh, don't worry about us, we're used to driving at night," Dremel said with a knowing wink, much like the ones Santa kept giving us.

"But, you haven't had a decent meal," I said. "Let me at least feed you …"

"Oh, you're very kind, but we need to get back on the road. We must get back on schedule. We've already missed too many gigs. The show must go on, you know," Dremel said.

"Oui," April chimed in. "We must get this show back on the road, no?"

"Great idea," Santa said. "Why don't you all pack up the van and let me talk to Charlie?"

"Absolutely," Dremel said, practically snapping to attention before starting to herd not only the French hens, but also Pat, out of the kitchen, despite Pat's protests.

As soon as they were gone, Santa turned to me. "I just wanted to thank you again for everything you did. Helping me, finding Dremel and the French hens, and even getting justice for Drexel."

"No thanks necessary, I was happy to do it," I said.

Santa smiled. "I know. Because deep down you're a good girl. I know you've done some naughty things in the past, but deep down, you're good."

There was something about his words and his manner that was very familiar. I felt like I was experiencing déjà vu. "Where did we meet? Was it back in New York?"

Santa's smile widened. "Why would we meet in New York?

You live in Redemption now." He moved a little closer to me, and I caught a whiff of his scent, sugar and spice and everything nice. "And really, Redemption is open to everyone. Even you."

Something flickered inside me, and just like that, a memory fell into place. "That was you, wasn't it? When I was looking for the lost Santa, you were the one I found, weren't you?"

Santa began to drift toward the door of the kitchen. "You have a good heart, Charlie. If you hang on to that, no matter what else happens, it's all going to be fine."

"But, wait a minute," I said. I had so many questions for him, like what happened that day and how could he possibly know the things he did, but before I could stop him, he had disappeared out the front door. I ran to the front door, flinging it open, but they were already gone.

"Where did they go?" I said to the white snow-covered yard. "Santa was just here. He had barely enough time to walk to the car much less for them to drive away."

"I don't know," Pat said behind me. "It's like they just … vanished."

I opened my mouth to answer, but before I could, I heard it. The faint noise as it seemed to float down from the heavens to us.

"Ho, ho, ho! Merry Christmas!"

A Note From Michele

Can't get enough of Charlie? I've got you covered. Keep going with *A Room For Murder*, coming October 2024!

And don't forget to check out audio! The entire series is available on Audible on audio. Or you can also start from the beginning with Book 1 *The Murder Before Christmas*.

A dead husband. A pregnant wife. A poisoned Christmas gift. Can Charlie discover the grinch who stole Christmas?

Grab your copy here:

MPWnovels.com/r/b3fxmaswide

***

You can also check out exclusive bonus content for the Charlie Kingsley Mystery series. Here's the link:

MPWnovels.com/r/b3fbonuswide

The bonus content reveals hints, clues, and sneak peeks you won't get just by reading the books, so you'll definitely want to take a look. You're going to discover a side of Redemption that is only available here.

***

If you enjoyed *Three French Hens and a Murder*, it would be wonderful if you would take a few minutes to leave a review and rating on Goodreads:

goodreads.com/book/show/202525628-three-french-hens-and-a-murder or Bookbub:

bookbub.com/books/three-french-hens-and-a-murder-a-charlie-kingsley-mysteries-novella-the-twelve-days-of-christmas-cozy-mysteries-book-3-by-michele-pw-pariza-wacek

(Feel free to follow me on any of those platforms as well.) I thank you and other readers will thank you (as your reviews will help other readers find my books.)

The *Charlie Kingsley Mysteries* series is a spin-off from my award-winning *Secrets of Redemption* series. *Secrets of Redemption* is a little different from the *Charlie Kingsley Mysteries*, as it's more psychological suspense, but it's still clean like a cozy.

You can learn more about both series, including how they fit together, at MPWNovels.com, along with lots of other fun things such as short stories, deleted scenes, giveaways, recipes, puzzles and more.

I've also included a sneak peek of *The Murder Before Christmas*, just turn the page to get started

Murder Before Christmas Chapter 1

"So, Courtney, is it?" I asked with what I hoped was a comforting and nonthreatening smile. I set the mug holding my newest tea blend I'd created for the Christmas season—a variety of fresh mint and a couple of other secret ingredients—down on the kitchen table. I called it "Candy Cane Concoctions", and hoped others would find it as soothing as it was refreshing. "What can I do for you?"

Courtney didn't look at me as she reached for her tea. She was young, younger than me, and extremely pretty, despite looking like something the cat dragged in. (And believe me, I know all about what cats can drag in. Midnight, my black cat, had presented me with more than my share of gifts over the years.) Courtney's long, wavy blonde hair was pulled back in a haphazard ponytail, and there were puffy, black circles under her china-blue eyes. She was also visibly pregnant.

"Well, Mrs. Kingsley," she began, but I quickly interrupted her.

"It's Miss, but please, call me Charlie." Yes, she was younger than me, but for goodness sake, not THAT much younger. Maybe it was time to start getting more serious about my morning makeup routine.

Her lips quirked up in a tiny smile that didn't quite reach her eyes. "Charlie, then. I was hoping you could make me a love potion."

I quickly dropped my gaze, busying myself by pushing the plate of frosted Christmas sugar cookies I had made earlier toward her, not wanting her to see my shock and sorrow. She was pregnant and wanted a love potion. This just couldn't be good.

"I don't actually do love potions," I said. "I make custom-blended teas and tinctures."

Her eyebrows knit together in confusion. "But people have been raving about how much you've helped them. Mrs. Witmore swears you cured her thyroid problems."

I tried not to sigh. "My teas and tinctures do have health benefits, that's true. Certain herbs and flowers can help with common ailments. In fact, for much of human civilization, there were no prescription drugs, so all they had to use were herbs and flowers. But I can't promise any cures."

"What about Ruthie?" Courtney asked. "She claims those heart tinctures you made are the reason Bob finally noticed her."

I gritted my teeth. When Ruthie's dad was recovering from a heart attack, I made a couple of teas and tinctures for him. Ruthie, who had a crush on her coworker Bob for years, was apparently so desperate for him to notice her that one day, she decided to bring one of my tinctures to work (I'm unclear which) and slip it into his drink. And apparently, shortly after that, Bob started up a conversation with her, and eventually asked her out on a date.

It didn't help matters that Jean, Ruthie's mother, had claimed my tinctures had reignited her and her husband's love life, which is probably how Ruthie got the idea to try them with Bob in the first place.

Needless to say, that was an unintended benefit.

"I didn't give Ruthie a love potion," I said. "I gave her dad some tinctures and teas to help his heart."

Courtney gazed at me with those clear-blue eyes, reminding me of a broken-down, worn-out doll. "Well, isn't that where love starts?"

"Maybe," I said. "But my intention was to heal her father's heart, not to make anyone fall in love with anyone else."

"But it worked," she said. "Can you just sell me whatever you gave her? I have money. I'll pay."

"It's not that simple," I said. "I really need to ask you some questions. It's always good to talk to your doctor, as well."

She bit her lip and dropped her gaze to the tea in her hands. She looked so lost and alone, I felt sorry for her.

"Why don't you tell me a little bit about who you want this love potion for?" I asked. "That would help me figure out how best to help you."

She didn't immediately answer, instead keeping her eyes down. Just as I was starting to think she wasn't going to say anything at all, she spoke. "It's for my husband," she said, her voice so low, it was nearly a whisper.

I could feel my heart sink to the floor. This was even more heartbreaking than I had imagined. "You think your husband fell out of love with you?"

"I know he has," she said. "He's having an affair."

"Oh Courtney," I sighed. "I'm so sorry to hear that."

She managed a tiny nod and picked up her tea to take a sip.

"Have you two talked about it?"

She shook her head quickly.

"Does he know you know?"

She shrugged.

"Maybe that's the place to start," I said, keeping my voice gentle. "Having a conversation."

"It won't help," she said, her voice still quiet.

"How do you know if you haven't tried?"

She didn't answer … just stared into her tea.

"Have you thought about marriage counseling?"

"He won't go." Her voice was firm.

"Have you asked?"

"I know. He's said before he thinks therapy is a waste of money."

"Okay. But you have a baby on the way," I said. "You need to be able to talk through things. I understand it might be difficult to talk about something like *this*, but …"

"He's in love with her." The words burst out of her as she raised her head. The expression on her face was so anguished that for a moment, it took my breath away.

"But how do you know if you haven't talked to him about it?"

"I just do," she said. "When you're married, you know these things. You can sense when your husband has fallen out of love with you. Hence, my need for a love potion. I need him to fall back in love with me. You can see how urgent this is." She gestured to her stomach. "In a few months, we're going to have a baby. I just *have* to get him to fall back in love with me."

Oh man, this was not going well. "I see why you would think that would be easier, but the problem is, there's no such thing as a love potion."

"Can you please just sell me what you made for Ruthie's dad? So I can at least try?"

"Whatever happened between Ruthie and Bob had nothing to do with one of my tinctures," I said flatly. "I don't want to give you false hope. I really think your best course of action is to have an open and honest conversation with him about the affair."

She was noticeably disappointed. It seemed to radiate out of every pore. I hated being the one to cause that, but I also wasn't going to sell her anything that could be misconstrued as a "love potion." Not only for her sake, but my own. The last thing I needed was lovesick women showing up at my door to buy something that didn't exist.

"Okay," she said quietly as she ducked her head so I couldn't quite see her face. "No love potion. How about the opposite?"

I looked at her in confusion. "The opposite?"

"Yes. Something that would kill him."

My mouth fell open. "Wha ... I'm sorry, could you repeat that?" I must have heard her wrong. She was still talking so quietly, not to mention hiding her face.

Courtney blinked and looked up at me. "I'm sorry?"

"I didn't hear what you said. Could you repeat it?"

"Oh. It was nothing." She offered an apologetic smile.

"No, really," I said. "I thought ..." I laughed a little self-consciously. "I thought you said you wanted something to kill your husband."

She blinked again. "Oh. Yeah. It was just a joke."

"A joke?"

"Yeah. I mean, you know. Sometimes married people want to kill each other. No big deal." Now it was her turn to let out a little twitter of laughter. "Have you ever been married?"

I shivered and put my hands around my mug to absorb the warmth. "No." Which was true. I had never been officially married, but that didn't mean my love life wasn't ... complicated.

Nor did it mean I didn't know exactly what she was talking about.

"Well, you know, sometimes married people can just get really angry with each other, and in the heat of the moment, even want to kill each other," she explained. "But they don't mean it. It's just because they love each other so much that sometimes that passion looks like something else. In the heat of the moment, in the middle of a fight, you can say all sorts of things you don't mean. But of course, they wouldn't *do* anything about it."

"Of course," I said. I decided not to mention that when she said it, she wasn't actually arguing with her husband. Nor did I bring up how perhaps she was protesting a bit too much.

I gave her a hard look as I sipped my tea.

She kept her gaze firmly on the table, refusing to meet my eyes. "Did I tell you how wonderful this blend is?" she asked. "It's so refreshing. Reminds me of a candy cane."

"Thanks. It's called 'Candy Cane Concoctions,' actually. I created it for the holidays," I said.

"It's wonderful." She took another hurried drink and put her mug down, tea sloshing over the side. "Are you selling it? Could I buy some?"

"Sure," I said, getting up from my chair. "Hang on a minute. I'll get you a bag."

She nodded as I left the kitchen to head upstairs to my office/work room. Although, to be fair, it was so small, it wasn't uncommon to find drying herbs or plants throughout the house.

I collected a bag and headed back to the kitchen. When I walked in, Courtney was standing up, fiddling with her purse. I instantly felt like something was off. Maybe it was the way she was standing or the bend of her neck, but she oozed guilt.

"Oh, there you are," she said, fishing out her wallet. "How much do I owe you?'

I told her, and she pulled out a wad of cash, handing me a twenty.

"I'll have to get you some change," I said.

"That's not necessary," she said, taking the bag. "You were so helpful to me, and besides, I need to get going."

"But this is way too much," I protested. "Just let me find my purse."

She waved me off as she left the kitchen and headed for the front door. "Nonsense. Truly, you were very helpful. No change is necessary." She jammed her arms into her coat, and without bothering to zip it up, opened the front door and headed out into the cold.

I closed the door after her, watching her through the window as she made her way down the driveway and into her car. She didn't seem very steady on her feet, and I wanted to make sure she got into her vehicle safely. After she drove off, I went back to the kitchen to look around.

Nothing appeared to be out of order. If she had been digging around looking for something (like something to kill her husband with), it wasn't obvious.

Still, I couldn't shake that uneasy feeling.

I went to the table to collect the dishes. Midnight strolled in as I was giving myself a pep talk.

"I'm sure she didn't mean it," I said to him. "She was probably just upset. I mean, she wasn't getting her love potion, and clearly, she was uncomfortable having a conversation with her husband. Although you'd think that would be a red flag."

Midnight sat down, his dark-green eyes studying me.

"Of course, that's hardly my business," I continued. "She's upset with him, and rightfully so. Who wouldn't be? Even if she wasn't actually joking in the moment, she was surely just letting off steam."

Midnight's tail twitched.

"Maybe this was even the first time she said it out loud," I said as I moved to the sink. "And now that she said it, she realized how awful it was. Of course she would never do anything like that." I turned to the cat. "Right?"

Midnight started cleaning himself.

"You're a lot of help," I muttered, turning back to the sink to finish the washing up.

As strange as that encounter was, it was likely the end of it.

I hoped.

Want to keep reading? Grab your copy of *The Murder Before Christmas* here:

MPWnovels.com/r/b3fxmaswide

Books and series by Michele Pariza Wacek

Charlie Kingsley Mysteries
(Cozy Mysteries)
See all of Charlie's adventures here.
https://MPWNovels.com/r/ck_3fh

Redemption Detective Agency
(Cozy Mysteries)
A spin-off from the Charlie Kingsley series.
https://MPWNovels.com/r/da_3fh

Secrets of Redemption series
(Pychological Thrillers)
The flagship series that started it all.
https://MPWnovels.com/r/rd_3fh

Mysteries of Redemption
(Psychological Thrillers)
A spin-off from the Secrets of Redemption series.
https://MPWnovels.com/r/mr_3fh

Riverview Mysteries
(standalone Pychological Thrillers)
These stories take place in Riverview, which is near Redemption.
https://MPWnovels.com/r/rm_3fh

Access your free exclusive bonus scenes from *A Wedding to Murder For* right here:
MPWnovels.com/r/b3fbonuswide

About Michele

A USA Today Bestselling, award-winning author, Michele taught herself to read at 3 years old because she wanted to write stories so badly. It took some time (and some detours) but she does spend much of her time writing stories now. Mystery stories, to be exact. They're clean and twisty, and range from psychological thrillers to cozies, with a dash of romance and supernatural thrown into the mix. If that wasn't enough, she posts lots of fun things on her blog, including short stories, puzzles, recipes and more, at MPWNovels.com.

Michele grew up in Wisconsin, (hence why all her books take place there), and still visits regularly, but she herself escaped the cold and now lives in the mountains of Prescott, Arizona with her husband and southern squirrel hunter Cassie.

When she's not writing, she's usually reading, hanging out with her dog, or watching the Food Network and imagining she's an awesome cook. (Spoiler alert, she's not. Luckily for the whole family, Mr. PW is in charge of the cooking.)

Made in the USA
Monee, IL
19 September 2024

66031325R00069